Stephen was kissing her like she'd never been kissed.

Nothing had ever felt this wonderful. His mouth was hard, yet oddly gentle on hers; his arms held her firmly, insistently, but with a certain unmistakable reverence. Every cell in her body vibrated with the sudden, inexplicable need to share herself with him—not just physically, but emotionally, too.

The kiss deepened, became harder, more demanding, heating Jill's blood. She tunneled her fingers through his thick, dark hair, unable to get enough of the feel of him, the rough and smooth of him.

With a hoarse moan Stephen broke the kiss, stepped away and looked at her. Like a window shade slowly lowering to hide the contents of a warm, inviting home, Stephen's expression gradually closed, and his eyes hardened.

"This will never happen again, Jill."

Dear Reader,

Silhouette Romance has a new look and we'd love to know if you like it! We've updated our covers, but inside you'll find the same heartwarming, satisfying love stories we know our readers look forward to each and every month. Silhouette Romance novels emphasize the traditional values of family, commitment... and the special kind of love that is destined to last forever. We hope our new covers say that to you.

Inside our bright new wrapping, you'll find delightful romances by Joleen Daniels, Val Whisenand and Pat Tracy. And in the spirit of our cover launch, we're introducing two talented newcomers to the line, Jude Randal and Jayne Addison.

In this month's WRITTEN IN THE STARS, we're featuring the steadfast Virgo man in Karen Leabo's *A Changed Man*. And in the months to come, watch for stories by your favorite authors, including Diana Palmer, Annette Broadrick, Marie Ferrarella and many, many more.

The Silhouette Romance authors and editors love to hear from readers and we'd love to hear from *you*.

Happy reading from all of us at Silhouette!

Valerie Susan Hayward
Senior Editor

A CHANGED MAN
Karen Leabo

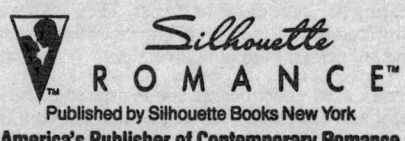

Published by Silhouette Books New York
America's Publisher of Contemporary Romance

If you purchased this book without a cover you should be aware that this book is stolen property. It was reported as "unsold and destroyed" to the publisher, and neither the author nor the publisher has received any payment for this "stripped book."

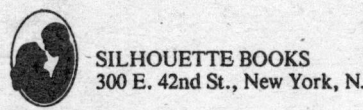

SILHOUETTE BOOKS
300 E. 42nd St., New York, N.Y. 10017

A CHANGED MAN

Copyright © 1992 by Karen Leabo

LOVE AND THE VIRGO MAN
Copyright © 1992 by Harlequin Enterprises B.V.

All rights reserved. Except for use in any review, the reproduction or utilization of this work in whole or in part in any form by any electronic, mechanical or other means, now known or hereafter invented, including xerography, photocopying and recording, or in any information storage or retrieval system, is forbidden without the permission of the publisher, Silhouette Books, 300 E. 42nd St., New York, N.Y. 10017

ISBN: 0-373-08886-8

First Silhouette Books printing September 1992

All the characters in this book have no existence outside the imagination of the author and have no relation whatsoever to anyone bearing the same name or names. They are not even distantly inspired by any individual known or unknown to the author, and all incidents are pure invention.

®: Trademark used under license and registered in the United States Patent and Trademark Office and in other countries.

Printed in the U.S.A.

Books by Karen Leabo

Silhouette Romance

Roses Have Thorns #648
Ten Days in Paradise #692
Domestic Bliss #707
Full Bloom #731
Smart Stuff #764
Runaway Bride #797
The Housewarming #848
A Changed Man #886

Silhouette Desire

Close Quarters #629
Lindy and the Law #676
Unearthly Delights #704

KAREN LEABO

I'm Sagittarius through and through, which means I insist on independence, love to travel—by plane, car or my own imagination—and hate to feel tied down to any one job, home or relationship. Naturally I'm not married. What man wants a wife who can't cook, is terrified of small children and who trots off at a moment's notice for snorkeling in the Bahamas or for an archaeological dig in Belize?

Oddly enough, I enjoyed challenging Jill, my free-spirited Sagittarian heroine, with an orderly, inflexible, but very lovable Virgo man. If Jill can work it out with Stephen, maybe there's hope for me!

VIRGO

Sixth sign of the Zodiac
August 23 to September 22
Symbol: Virgin
Planet: Mercury
Element: Earth
Stone: Sapphire
Color: Navy Blue, White
Metal: Mercury
Flower: Aster
Lucky Day: Wednesday
Countries: Brazil, Turkey, Switzerland
Cities: Los Angeles, Paris, Washington, D.C.

Famous Virgos

Bill Murray
Michael Jackson
Sean Connery
Larry Hagman

Lily Tomlin
Gloria Estefan
Greta Garbo
Lauren Bacall

★

Chapter One

Jill Ballantine threw a murderous glance at her ringing telephone, wishing her potent glare could silence it. The 800 number she'd installed was doing everything the phone company had promised—and more. Her mail-order spice business was swamped with new members, and Jill was sinking fast.

She let the telephone ring once more before lunging for the receiver. "Good morning, can I spice up your life?"

"Jilly, thank heavens you're home. I'm having a little problem, and I need you to..."

Jill couldn't quite catch the rest of the sentence. She used her elbow to close the door that led out to her glassed-in sunroom, where more than a dozen bird cages hung from the ceiling. "What did you say, Aunt Pauline? I couldn't hear you over the birds."

"You have to come over, right away. I need you. This is serious."

Jill thought longingly of the leftover pizza warming in the oven. Her stomach growled menacingly. "All right, Auntie, don't pop your garters. I'll be right over, as soon as I finish filling this batch of orders."

"Now! It can't wait."

Jill curbed the impatient sigh that threatened to erupt. Her Aunt Pauline was a dear, but sometimes the woman's flair for melodrama was a nuisance. "I'm coming, soon as I hang up the phone."

She placed a stopper in the tiny crystal jar she'd just filled, then set it with the dozens of others she'd already processed that morning. Glancing at the empty jars still to be dealt with, she indulged in the sigh she'd repressed moments ago. At the rate she was going, it would take her all day just to complete the current club members' monthly shipments, and she had a six-inch stack of new orders to process.

November's spice was nutmeg, and its pungent odor filled her small apartment—the former servants' quarters of her aunt's house—lending the illusion that a frenzy of holiday baking was going on. But baking was a luxury Jill seldom indulged in these days. The way things were going, she would be lucky if she found the time to heat up a turkey pot pie for Thanksgiving dinner. She still had bird cages to clean and Mrs. Rowan's lawn to mow before it rained.

"Ah, well, someday I'll get caught up," Jill murmured as she stripped off her plastic gloves. She switched on her answering machine, then stepped out into the deceptively warm, moist day. Even the concrete beneath her bare feet was warm.

Who would guess it was November? she thought as she walked across the carport that separated her quarters from the sprawling pink stucco house her aunt occupied. Although Jill loved Southern California, her eternally sunny home for the past two years, she did miss the bright fall leaves and crisp autumn air of Massachusetts.

She entered the house through the kitchen door. A pair of garrishly feathered finches chirped a greeting from their cage on top of the refrigerator. Water boiled briskly in a copper kettle on the stove, but her aunt was nowhere in sight. Jill turned down the heat. "Aunt Pauline?"

"In here, Jilly Bean."

Jill followed the sound of her aunt's high-pitched voice, wincing at the family nickname she couldn't seem to shake. When she reached the living room she skidded to a halt. A strange man stood in the middle of the pink braided rug. *Or maybe not so strange,* she thought as the man's perfectly sculpted features struck a cord of familiarity.

"Stevie?"

"Stephen," he corrected her, looking down his aquiline nose at her with cool gray eyes. "You must be Jill."

Then this *was* her cousin Stevie Whitfield, from Wisconsin. Well, not actually her real cousin. Her Uncle Jigs, who had died two years ago, had been married to Pauline, Stephen's aunt. The two "cousins" had often collided at the many family gatherings held here, in this house. But Stephen's visits had become less frequent in recent years. Jill hadn't seen him for at least a decade.

A lot could change in ten years, she mused with an inner smile. The tall, skinny, bespectacled teenager she remembered had grown into a devastatingly handsome man. One thing hadn't changed, however, and that was the way he looked at her—as if she were an especially repugnant species of insect that the exterminators had somehow missed.

That cool gaze had always managed to make her feel inadequate, somehow, and today was no exception. She glanced down at her faded red T-shirt, the souvenir of a long-ago rock concert, and her white shorts streaked with tan smudges from the nutmeg she'd been handling all morning. She knew without benefit of a mirror that her hair formed an unruly reddish cloud around her head, and she hadn't bothered with makeup. Belatedly she wished she'd at least put on her shoes; her bare feet made her feel ridiculously vulnerable.

Finally she looked at Pauline, who sat on the edge of her floral brocade settee, her lips pressed tightly together in a thin line. Jill hadn't seen her aunt looking so grim since Jigs's funeral.

"What's going on, Auntie?" she asked as she crossed the room to sit beside the suddenly frail-looking older woman. Jill put an arm around Pauline's thin shoulders.

"Oh, Jilly Bean, I'm afraid I'm really up a creek this time."

She already knew enough about him to dislike him and really didn't care to learn any more. He was an uptight control freak. As a kid, he'd taken pride in winning every game he played, from touch football to Chinese checkers. If they were watching TV, the remote control was always in his hand. Even the sand castles he had built at the beach were constructed with rigid angles, architecturally correct down to the crenellations on the towers.

Jill had relished her childhood visits with Pauline and Jigs. This had been the one place she could be herself, drop her guard without having to constantly answer to anyone. But with Stephen around, she'd felt as self-conscious as she had around her doting, often demanding parents. They'd expected so much from her, and it seemed she had constantly disappointed them. She'd never measured up to Stephen's rigid expectations, either.

In short, he'd been a real wet blanket.

He couldn't be much different now. After all, he crunched numbers for a living. His khaki slacks and white button-down shirt were neatly pressed and tailored to fit his muscular frame to perfection. His strong jaw was closely shaven, and his freshly trimmed, dark brown hair showed no signs of having been tousled by the ocean breeze. Everything about him screamed tight control.

"Yes, you two have a nice chat," Pauline agreed with a tentative smile, though her brow was knitted into telltale wrinkles of worry. "This won't take a minute." She bustled into the kitchen, leaving the two "cousins" alone.

The air fairly crackled with the man's disapproval toward Jill, and she wondered what she'd done to earn it.

"So what's the problem?" she said, coming right to the point.

"What's the problem?" he repeated, incredulous. "Pauline has obviously been living far beyond her means, and you wonder what's the problem? You were supposed to be keeping an eye on her! That's why you're here, living in an oceanside resort town in a luxurious house with free room and board. The family entrusted you to take care of things for her. How could you allow her to spend money so irresponsibly?"

Jill straightened to her full five foot five, bristling with indignation. "You really ought to get the facts straight before you go making accusations," she countered, her hands balling into fists. How dare he? "What's the matter, Stevie, are you afraid there'll be nothing left for you to inherit?" It was a low blow, but nothing less than he deserved.

"That's *Stephen*," he corrected again. "I haven't gone by Stevie since high school. And just what are the facts, Jilly Bean?"

"I'll make a deal with you: I won't call you Stevie if you won't call me Jilly Bean. And the facts, cous, are these—first off, I don't recall you or anyone else volunteering to live with Aunt Pauline. It isn't some wonderful privilege your family granted me. When Uncle Jigs died, no one else could take time off from their busy, busy lives to look after her. I was drafted.

"Second, I'm not living here on your aunt's charity. I pay her a reasonable rent for the use of her servants' quarters, and I cook my own meals in my own kitchen. In addition, I take care of the grounds. I mow the lawn, trim the shrubs, plant the flowers and weed the flowerbeds, and I keep the pool clean, among other things.

"Third, I am Pauline's friend and companion, not her prison warden, not even her guardian. It isn't my place to decide what she buys with her money. However," Jill hastened to add, "since I do spend a great deal of time with her, I can assure you with some degree of confidence that she hasn't been living extravagantly. In fact, over the past few months she seems to have really pulled herself together. This shortage of funds has to be some mistake, some computer error or something. And when I find out who's responsible, I'm going to flatten them. Auntie doesn't need to worry like this."

Stephen glanced at his watch, seemingly unperturbed. "Are you about done?"

"For now."

"Thank God." He took a deep breath, as if marshaling his thoughts. "Your points are well taken. I suppose I shouldn't have jumped on you like that."

Jill made a concerted effort to calm herself. "That's not much of an apology, but I'll take what I can get. You don't apologize very often, do you."

"I don't often find myself in the wrong."

Oh, brother. Would she love to take this guy down a peg or two!

"I'm very fond of Aunt Pauline," he said. "I just want to help her, that's all."

"Then why are we arguing?" she countered. "We're on the same side. And if you're so fond of her, why weren't you at Uncle Jigs's funeral?"

"I was in the hospital at the time."

"Oh." Now she was the one jumping to conclusions. She hated to be wrong, probably as much as Stephen did. "Ulcers?"

He looked surprised at that, the first genuine emotion she'd seen him reveal. "How did you know that?"

You're the type, she wanted to say. Instead she mumbled, "I'm sure Auntie told me."

He sighed, stuck his hands in his pockets, and stared down at the shiny leather toes of his loafers. "I really am sorry," he said, in a voice so low she could hardly make it out. "I guess I just wanted to blame someone for this, this inconvenience, and you made a quick and easy target."

"Forget it," she said, though she wasn't sure if she was quite ready to forgive.

"Why don't you go see what's keeping Pauline?" he suggested. "I need to get some things out of my car. Looks like I'll be here for a while."

Jill was all too happy to escape Stephen's unsettling presence for a few minutes. She found her aunt in the fifties-style pink and aqua kitchen, still dithering over which tea to serve and whether she should offer Stephen sugar, honey or artificial sweetener.

"Serve him the Earl Gray," Jill said. "And he probably takes it plain." *If he drinks tea at all,* she added silently. Somehow, Stephen didn't seem like the tea type.

"It doesn't matter that much, I suppose," Pauline said as she arranged cups, saucers and a sugar bowl on a serving tray. She poured the boiling water from the kettle into a china tea pot and set it, too, on the tray.

"I'll get it," Jill offered. "That looks heavy."

"Leave it be for just a minute, Jilly," Pauline said as she pulled a chair out from the kitchen table. "Sit down. I have to talk to you. I would have done this sooner if I'd known Stephen would be here so quickly. Then he insisted on seeing you the moment he walked in the door, so I didn't get the chance to warn you."

Jill sat obediently in the chair as Pauline took the one across from her, then waited patiently for her aunt to reveal whatever was on her mind.

"It's about Stevie—Stephen, I guess we call him now. I really didn't want him to come."

"I wish you'd talked to me first," Jill agreed. "Maybe we could have figured something out without involving the rest of the family."

"You mean about the money?" Pauline waved away that problem as if it were nothing more than a pesky mosquito. "Oh, I'm sure Stephen will take care of it, better than either of us could. He's quite qualified. No, it's him *personally* that I'm worried about."

"Does he make you uncomfortable?" Jill asked.

"Not me, dear. You. Stephen and you." She shook her head. "Bad news. Very bad news."

"Auntie, stop being mysterious and come to the point. He's a bit of a stuffed shirt, I'll grant you that, but I can handle him." She had just proved that, to her own satisfaction, at least.

"I suppose I'd better start at the beginning," Pauline said, casting a worried glance through the kitchen door. "I'll try to make it fast."

"Please."

"It goes back to Madame Zoey. You remember her, don't you?"

Jill refrained from rolling her eyes. "How could I forget the amazing Madame Zoey? You're not seeing her again, are you? Pauline, you promised me you wouldn't give any more money to that rip-off artist."

"I haven't seen her in several weeks, but she's not a rip-off artist," Pauline said in an injured tone. "Remember, she predicted the day when Jigs would die."

"Anyone could have predicted that. He was a very sick man," Jill argued. It was that one lucky guess that had caused Pauline to become so devoted to the phony psychic. "But go on. What does she have to do with the present situation?"

"The last time I saw her she mentioned you—with no prompting from me, mind you. I wanted to speak to the ghost of Errol Flynn, but she wouldn't listen. She kept insisting that you were headed for trouble. It was most odd."

Jill had to agree. She suspected that Madame Zoey usually told her wealthy pigeons exactly what they wanted to hear. "So what did she say?"

"She said that you should be on your guard, that a man was going to cause you great pain and sorrow."

Jill couldn't help letting a small snort of laughter escape. "Aunt Pauline," she said, "*all* men cause great pain and sorrow. It's part of their genetic makeup."

But Pauline refused to be humored. "She said you must beware the Virgo man. I didn't think much of it at the time because I was miffed over missing Errol, and you didn't have any men in your life, anyway."

"More's the pity," Jill murmured.

"The *Virgo* man, don't you see?" Pauline grabbed on to Jill's forearm with surprising strength. "Stephen is a Virgo."

"Is that what you're worried about? I can think of a lot of reasons to beware of Stephen, but none of them have to do with his astrological sign," Jill said, trying to allay her aunt's irrational fears.

"But a Virgo man and a Sagittarian woman can cause nothing but trouble for each other—"

"Auntie, he's not going to cause *me* any trouble. You're the one who has to beware. He'll be delving into your personal affairs, remember. Next thing you know, he'll be putting you on an allowance and scrutinizing every check you write."

"Do you really think so?"

"Look, let's not buy trouble where there isn't any. I'm sure that when Stephen goes over the records he'll find the problem and everything will be fine. Meanwhile we'll just have to put up with him. It can't take more than a few days, right? How much pain and sorrow could ol' Mr. Virgo cause in such a short time?"

Silently, Jill answered her own question. *A lot.* She had her reservations about this interloper, despite her outward show of bravado.

"I suppose I'd better serve the tea before it gets cold," Pauline said with an absent gesture.

"Right," Jill agreed as she stood and retrieved the tray. She heard the front door open and close, indicating Stephen's return.

The pair of birds on top of the refrigerator flapped in agitation at the noise, and Pauline soothed them with a soft clicking noise she made with her tongue. "What's troubling them?" she wondered aloud.

The answer to that question was painfully obvious as soon as the two women entered the living room. There, surveying the world from Stephen's arms, was the hugest, ugliest cat Jill had ever seen, with mangy-looking black fur, stubby, notched ears, and malevolent orange eyes.

Jill and Pauline exchanged worried glances. "I'll take the birds to my place," Jill said as she set the tray down on the coffee table.

Stephen looked up, only then noticing their presence. "Birds?"

"Finches," Pauline explained as she approached her nephew and the cat warily. "They're Jill's birds, actually. She brought them over here, away from all the others, thinking they might be more successful at breeding if they had some peace and quiet."

"Breeding?"

"I raise finches," Jill explained defensively. "This pair happens to be a somewhat rare species, and they're going to die of heart attacks if they see that cat. Excuse me." She returned to the kitchen and lifted the cage from its place on top of the refrigerator, thinking that it was rather presumptuous of Stephen to bring his cat without asking.

She liked cats all right. In fact, there wasn't an animal in the world that Jill didn't have some affinity for. But cats weren't compatible with birds. If she were to have any pets besides the finches, she'd prefer a big, floppy, slobbery dog. Now there was a sincere, straightforward animal.

By the time she returned from her apartment, the cat was sitting docilely in Pauline's lap, purring. Stephen sat next to her on the settee.

"He's a rather nice animal, Jilly," Pauline said. "Come give him a pat."

Jill dutifully stepped forward and scratched the cat behind its battle-scarred ears. It eyed her disdainfully.

"I would have boarded him," Stephen explained, "but the vet couldn't take him on such short notice. So I brought him with me."

"Couldn't you find someone to take care of him?" Jill asked. "A neighbor? Seems kind of strange to drag him halfway across the country."

Stephen stiffened. "I don't have any close neighbors. Anyway, he's recovering from an accident, and I didn't want to leave him with just anyone. I can find a vet in Del Rosa if you don't want him here."

"That's an excellent idea," Jill said, just as Pauline exclaimed that of course the sweet kitty could stay here.

Stephen looked up at Jill then, an unmistakable glint of triumph in his gray eyes. That made her remember something else about him that was infuriating. As a kid he was always competing for Pauline's favor, seeking her approval.

"What sort of accident did he have?" Jill couldn't help asking. She hated the thought of any creature in pain, even this unfriendly beast.

"He was hit by a car in front of my house and left to die," Stephen replied, bitterness hardening his voice. "I had to take him in. It's not like I really wanted a cat, but I've got one, at least until he's well and I can find him another home."

"Well, I guess I don't mind him staying here," Jill said grudgingly. So the man did have a soft spot. She never would have guessed. "Just so long as you keep him away from my finches."

"Boniface is very well behaved," Stephen assured her.

She didn't doubt it. A man like him wouldn't own an unruly pet. The cat was probably neutered and declawed. She would be surprised if he dared to even shed.

"Sit down, Jill," Pauline said, indicating with a regal gesture the spot next to her on the settee. "You make me nervous, pacing about like that. Drink your tea."

Jill chose instead a rose-patterned wingback chair, a safe distance from Stephen, who was even more difficult to read than his pet. "So, how is it that you were able to get away from your accounting business on such short notice?" she asked him as she stirred sugar into her tea.

"It's a slow time of year," he answered. "My partner can cover for me. Anyway, I'm due a vacation."

"You call straightening out someone's financial affairs a vacation?" she couldn't help asking.

"It's a change of pace, at any rate," he said. "And your California sunshine does hold a certain allure. There's a foot of snow on the ground in Madison. I wouldn't mind seeing the beach. If I take an hour or two off, you won't mind showing me around, will you?" The question was faintly challenging, as if he was deliberately baiting her.

Pauline looked horrified. "Oh, now, that would never do," she said quickly. "Jill is much too busy to be playing tour guide, right, Jill? She has her own company, you know, and it takes up, oh, just all of her time."

Jill found herself nodding in agreement, although she almost regretted doing so. The prospect of getting the stiff and proper Stephen Whitfield on a public beach and loosening him up with a rousing game of volleyball seemed oddly appealing. "Very busy," she murmured, wondering how the man would look in a swimsuit. She took a gulp of tea, disconcerted over her errant line of thinking.

"Oh, really? What kind of business?" Stephen asked.

"Just a little mail order thing," she answered. "And the finches, too. I sell them to pet stores."

The cat picked that moment to jump off Pauline's lap, thankfully distracting everyone away from the subject of Jill's business. Spice Up Your Life, Inc. was in its infancy, and she was still making mistakes—like underestimating the response she would get from that last ad in *Southern Cooking* magazine. She didn't want to share anything about her mail-order outfit with Stephen. He probably dealt with large corporations on a daily basis, and he would just think her efforts were silly.

She couldn't bear to have anyone laugh at her, not this time.

Her track record in the business world wasn't exactly enviable. She despised full-time employment—part of her Sagittarian makeup, her aunt had told her—and thus had tried all kinds of get-rich-quick schemes in order to avoid a nine-to-five job. All of them had flopped miserably, including the finches. She'd paid a hefty sum for the pair of exotic Lady Goulds, and the perverse little birds refused to breed.

But her spice venture was going to work—she knew it in her bones. Until she got all the bugs worked out, however, she didn't want anyone making fun of it, or her. For once she was going to do something right, and she was going to do it on her own.

"Boniface, get down from there," Stephen scolded when the cat jumped on Pauline's crowded bookcase.

"Oh, let him explore," Pauline said, unconcerned. "He can't hurt anything—" Her sentence was cut short when the cat leapt to the top shelf, dislodging a half-dozen books that came crashing to the floor. The entire case rocked menacingly.

Jill and Stephen jumped to their feet at the same time. Stephen lunged for the cat while Jill held the bookcase steady. Another avalanche of books came crashing down, narrowly missing her head.

"Well behaved, eh?" she couldn't help whispering as he made a grab for the cat, which darted agilely out of his grasp, leapt to the floor and slunk into the dining room and under the buffet.

"He's just disoriented," Stephen said apologetically as he bent to retrieve a handful of books from the floor. "He'll settle down in a while."

Jill, too, began gathering up the fallen books. When they both reached for the same paperback, a short tug-of-war ensued before Stephen relinquished his hold.

"I'll take care of the mess," he told her. "Go sit down and finish your tea."

"I really need to get back to work," she said. "Auntie, you call if you need me. I'm just a few steps away." But she looked directly at Stephen as she spoke these words, giving him a silent warning: *Treat her gently*.

She made a brisk exit, realizing as she entered her own quarters that she still held in her hand the book she and Stephen had tussled over. She noted the cover absently, then did a double take as the title registered: *Astrology for the Beginner*. With a thoughtful frown, she took the book into her bedroom, flipping through the pages as she went. Gemini, Cancer, Leo, ah, there it was, Virgo—the Virgin.

She snickered. Stephen, a virgin? Not possible. He was too... too... something.

She bent down the corner of the page, then closed the book and set it on the nightstand. Not that she believed in any of this mumbo-jumbo, but it couldn't hurt to at least read up on the Virgo male. Maybe she would learn a trick or two that would help her keep him in line.

Chapter Two

"You call these records?" Stephen bellowed, making a sweeping gesture with his hand to encompass the various boxes, shopping bags and rubber-band-wrapped piles on Pauline's dining room table. But when his aunt winced at his outburst, he was immediately contrite. "Sorry, I didn't mean to yell. But how can you live like this? It'll take me at least a full day just to get this stuff sorted. Don't you ever balance your checkbook?"

Pauline shrugged her thin shoulders helplessly. "Jigs always took care of those things. And since he died, if I wanted to know how much money was in my account, I just called that nice Mr. Kingston at the bank. Only he wasn't so nice last time he called," she said with a huff.

"Well, it's no matter," Stephen said, feeling worse and worse for having raised his voice, especially when

Pauline crept out of the room as if fearing to earn his wrath again. Poor Aunt Pauline. It wasn't her fault, not really. Lots of people were disorganized.

It was that darn cousin Jill making him cranky. The moment he'd seen her, it all came crashing back—knock-knees, braces, red pigtails and a mouth that wouldn't quit. She was always getting in trouble, dashing off in twenty different directions at once. She would leave projects unfinished or jump up in the middle of a Monopoly game—usually when she was losing—suddenly unable to postpone a trip to the beach.

Time had taken care of the knees and the teeth, and her hair was a softer color now. In fact, it reminded him of cinnamon, just like the dusting of freckles across her nose. But she was still mouthy as hell. It made him edgy just knowing she was within a hundred feet of him.

Although he'd at first suspected that his dear "cousin" had somehow wormed her way into Pauline's confidence and made off with her fortune, he'd known almost instantly upon seeing Jill again that she was no crook. Her eyes, the frankest sky-blue eyes he'd ever seen, had told him that.

But even this assumption about her made him uncomfortable. He wasn't accustomed to relying on such flimsy, intuitive evidence. He was a man of facts.

She might be innocent, but that didn't mean she wasn't negligent. She really should have been keeping a closer eye on Pauline's expenditures.

With a sigh of resignation, he dug into the pile of papers. Ordinarily he loved creating order from chaos, but on this occasion he was worried about what he might find. After Jigs had died, there was some question as to Pauline's mental stability, which is exactly why Jill had been chosen—drafted—to look after the older woman. And though Pauline seemed perfectly lucid on the surface, she *could* be nutty as peanut brittle and hiding it well. She might have let that money run through her hands, spending it irrationally. If that's what had happened, steps would have to be taken—unpleasant steps.

On the other hand, it was entirely possible that she had simply misplaced the money—stashed it in another bank account and forgotten it. He had dealt with an estate once where the deceased had hidden money in twenty-seven different accounts. Then there was always a chance, though a remote one, that the bank had made an error.

The sorting didn't take as long as Stephen had feared, and by noon he had the papers roughly organized and was ready to take a closer look. But first he had to have lunch. If there was one thing he could say about his metabolism, it was that he had an infallible biological clock. If he didn't have breakfast at seven, lunch at noon and dinner at six-thirty, his body protested.

"Pauline?" he called out, figuring his aunt was somewhere about the house, though he hadn't seen or heard her lately. "What do you want to do about lunch?"

He received no answer, but he heard someone whisk open the kitchen screen door, then let it slam shut.

"Pauline?" he called again.

"No, it's me," Jill answered.

He turned to look at her as she breezed toward him, and he liked what he saw. Her summery blouse, with its puffy sleeves and lace collar and delicate rose print, dipped low at the neckline, revealing a complement of cinnamon freckles and just a hint of shadow between her breasts. She'd acquired cleavage some time during the past ten years, he mused, suppressing a grin. Last night's baggy T-shirt hadn't revealed that development. The blouse was tucked into pale blue jeans that clung snugly to her racehorse legs.

He smiled a greeting, determined not to let her rub him the wrong way. Maybe they could even start fresh today.

"So how's it going?" she asked. "Find out anything?"

He shook his head. "Not yet. It's a mess."

"Well I hope you haven't been too hard on poor Auntie," she said with a worried frown.

"I haven't had the opportunity. She's made herself scarce. In fact, I don't think she's at home."

"Really?" Jill stepped into the living room to look out the window. "Hmm, that's odd. Her car's gone. She usually lets me know when she's going out. Oh, well. I was on my way to the deli for lunch and I came over to see if you and Pauline were hungry."

"Actually I am. Your timing is perfect."

Her sudden smile surprised him and short-circuited his normally organized thought processes for a few moments, until he realized he was staring stupidly at her, basking in the warmth of her good humor. It was the first real smile she'd awarded him.

"Um, lunch, yes," he murmured as he uncapped his gold fountain pen, eager to busy himself. He made a few hasty notations on the top sheet of his as-yet-unused legal pad, then tore the page off and handed it to her.

She stared at it uncomprehendingly.

"Can't you read my handwriting? It says smoked turkey and baby Swiss on rye, with mustard—mild, not hot—lettuce, tomato, and absolutely no pickles. Is...is something wrong? This isn't one of those weird California delis where I have to order avocado and kiwi fruit on sunflower seed bread, is it?"

"Um, no, it's just a regular deli," she replied distractedly as she folded the paper and stuck it in her jeans pocket.

"Oh, the money, of course," he said, thinking that's why she hesitated. He reached into his trouser pocket and produced a gold money clip, from which he peeled off a couple of bills. "This should cover it," he said as he handed the money to her.

She accepted it, then was suddenly full of purpose. "Well, I guess I'll go, then. If Pauline comes back, tell her I'm getting her a sandwich, too. She can save it for later if she doesn't want it now."

Jill left the same way she came, with a whisk and a slam of the kitchen door, and Stephen felt suddenly, irrationally, bereft of her company. For Pete's sake, she'd only been in his presence a minute or so. But there was something very sunny and warm about her, something that hadn't come through yesterday. Then again, yesterday they'd been circling each other warily like a couple of roosters eager for a fight. Today, mellowed by a good night's sleep, perhaps, she reminded him of Southern California itself. Belatedly he wished he'd gone with her. He was feeling kind of cooped up in here with all these numbers, and he was on vacation, after all.

A sharp, painful sensation in his calf grabbed his attention. "Boniface, you savage, get your claws out of my leg." The cat had an unfortunate habit of making a bid for attention in the most obnoxious manner possible. Usually it was a well-placed set of needle-sharp claws. "You're hungry, right? I can take a hint."

Boniface relinquished his hold on Stephen's calf and wrapped himself around his ankle instead, purring rapturously. His affection could mean only one thing.

Stephen disengaged his leg and went into the kitchen to open a can of food. He'd tried to feed the cat this morning but hadn't been able to locate him. Surprisingly, Boniface seemed uninterested in the fishy-smelling fare his master offered to him. Instead he went right to the screen door, then pushed his bulky body through a torn corner of the nylon mesh.

"So, that's where you've been." Stephen followed the cat outside, intending to catch him and confine him in the house where he couldn't get into trouble. But Boniface didn't want to be caught, and he led Stephen a merry chase through well-manicured flower beds and shrubs, all the way to the back of the servants' quarters.

That's when the cat's true aim became apparent. He stretched up to peer through a wall of windows into a sun room—Jill's sun room. Bird cages, at least a dozen, were suspended from the ceiling, housing a veritable smorgasbord of finches.

Stephen lunged for the cat, catching him this time. "Oh, no you don't," he scolded as he carried the squirming animal back inside. "Jill would skin you and then me if you upset her precious birds. So stop licking your chops."

As soon as they were back in the kitchen, Boniface leapt from Stephen's arms, gave him a look of supreme insult and stalked away.

Stephen just shook his head. He hadn't wanted the damn cat and had fully intended to find it another home as soon as it was well. But the bad-tempered feline had somehow wormed its way into his affections. Giving him away now would be like putting an ugly, ill-mannered child up for adoption.

Stephen returned to the dining room, deciding to start with the bank statements. He went back two years, to the time Uncle Jigs had died, and worked his way forward, figuring that whatever went wrong happened after that date.

At first nothing appeared out of the ordinary. He was appalled by the expenses involved with the upkeep of this house, but that was to be expected, he supposed. California wasn't cheap. There were regular, monthly deposits made to the checking account, representing the profits from Jigs's investment portfolio fund, Stephen figured. Pauline appeared to be living within her means.

But about the fifth month, something curious began to appear. The deposits got bigger. And so did the weekly checks to a D.Z. Ryzinski.

Stephen went back through each of the canceled checks, setting aside all that were made out to this Ryzinski person. He'd noted the name earlier and had assumed it belonged to a cleaning lady or a yard worker. The amounts had been small, thirty-five or forty dollars. But gradually the payments had escalated, until Pauline was paying out thousands of dollars per month.

Blackmail? That was Stephen's first thought. But what could a sweet little old lady like Pauline have to hide? It was more likely she'd been somehow tricked into writing those checks. Regardless, he couldn't think of anything that would account for the legitimate payout of that much money. Here, then, was the answer to the missing quarter million.

No wonder his aunt had left the house that morning. She knew, and had known all along, what Stephen would find when he started delving into her records. And she knew there would be hell to pay.

Discovering the source of the lost money had been easy, much easier than Stephen had anticipated. Ferreting out the story behind these checks, however, was probably going to be a bit more difficult. And recovering the money, probably impossible.

Jill sat outside under a pink-and-white-striped umbrella, savoring each bite of her peanut butter and banana sandwich as she reviewed what she'd learned about Stephen—theoretically—from the astrology book.

She'd taken the book to bed last night, intending to read a few pages to put her to sleep. But the section on the Virgo male had proved fascinating, engrossing reading. She'd actually found herself laughing out loud at some of the typical Virgo characteristics, which fit Stephen to a T.

Neat and tidy. Even as a kid, his clothes had always been meticulously laundered and pressed, his hair combed, his shoes clean. At the beach, when everyone else was sunburned and windblown, he looked as if he'd just walked off the pages of a sportswear catalogue.

Careful with money. Jill couldn't remember him ever blowing money like she did, on ice cream or at the video arcade, yet he always seemed to have cash when he really wanted something.

Critical and analytical. That was what she remembered most about him. No matter what she tried—and she tried lots of things, from oil painting to gardening to cooking—he had offered his unsolicited critique. His opinions weren't given in a mean-spirited way; in fact, he had always seemed eager to be of service, pointing out the positive as well as the negative. But that helpful attitude hadn't softened her irritation with him one iota.

Yes, Stephen was a Virgo, all right. She'd gone to sleep last night with a modicum more faith in astrology than she'd had before.

This morning she had deliberately set out to get on Stephen's good side, using her newfound knowledge. She'd wanted to convince him to have lunch with her, intending to bury the hatchet. It seemed important that the two of them put aside their childhood differences and learn to get along, or at least tolerate each other. They were both on the same side, after all—they both wanted to get Pauline out of a jam. How could they help her if they were at odds?

So Jill had put on a seldom-worn Laura Ashley blouse instead of one of her usual T-shirts, even though she wasn't crazy about puffs and lace, because the book had emphasized the Virgo's fondness for a neat appearance. She had applied makeup, combed her hair as best she could and had even filed her nails. And for what?

She'd felt an illogical flutter of happiness when Stephen had agreed to lunch. And then she'd come down to earth with a painful plunk. He didn't want her to be his dining companion, he wanted her to be his catering service, his errand girl.

Still, she had to chuckle at the way he'd placed his order. He was so precise. Not a moment of hesitation, and he definitely did *not* want pickles. He would probably look at the receipt and count his change, too. She would shortchange him by one penny just to see if he'd say anything, she decided with a mischievous grin as she pulled her jeep into the driveway a few minutes later.

Her grin faded when she entered the house. She immediately sensed a change in the atmosphere, and within a second or two of opening the kitchen door she was assaulted by Stephen's loud and very angry voice.

"Jill, get in here!"

The nerve of him! "Hey, I know I'm a little late with your lunch but you don't have to—" She cut herself off. Lunch, or lack thereof, had nothing to do with Stephen's mood. As soon as she entered the dining room he stood and turned toward her, a black look on his face, and waved a handful of checks under her nose.

"Who the devil is D. Z. Ryzinski?"

Jill straightened her spine. "Ask politely and I might answer," she said coolly as she stepped past him to drop the white deli sack on top of his legal pad. The puff of breeze created by the impact caused several papers to flutter out of order.

Stephen laid the checks down on the table and pushed his dark hair off his forehead, obviously reaching for calmness. The gesture was one she remembered well. He used to do that whenever she tried his patience—like on the rare occasions when she'd beaten him at cards, or the time she'd spilled cherry soda on his white shirt. And the cool, superior look that came afterward, once he'd mastered his temper, used to make her quiver in her sandals.

The Look, as she called it, didn't have quite the same effect now that she was grown up. In fact, those quicksilver gray eyes did make her quiver inside, but not with apprehension. She'd done nothing to merit his disapproval, after all, so what did she have to fear?

"If you please," he said slowly, in a lower tone of voice, "who is D. Z. Ryzinski?"

"That's much better. And I haven't the faintest notion. Why?"

"Because Pauline has paid out tens of thousands of dollars to him or her over the past two years, on an almost biweekly basis. That's where her missing quarter million dollars went. I haven't accounted for all of it yet, but I haven't been through the last few bank statements. You honestly don't know who Ryzinski is?" In the span of a few seconds Stephen had abandoned his irate stance and seemed to genuinely be asking for help.

For Pauline's sake Jill made a concerted effort to overlook his brief spurt of temper and tried to match an identity with the name. She scratched her head and sucked on her lower lip while she thought about it. "Ryzinski, Ryzinski...it does sound familiar, I'll have to admit."

Stephen flipped over one of the checks. "Some of the earlier checks were paid out to an account at a Santa Barbara bank. Does that help?"

The pieces of information whirled in her mind for a moment, then clicked into focus. "Madame Zoey!"

"Who?"

"Aunt Pauline's psychic. She lives in Santa Barbara. Sure, that has to be it!"

Rather than being pleased with her deduction, Stephen drew his dark brows together as his eyes once again reflected the color of thunderclouds. "You let Pauline throw her fortune away on some phony crystal ball reader?"

"It wasn't like that!"

"Oh? And I suppose you believe in this...what did you say her name was? Madame Zoey?"

"No, of course I don't believe in it. But Pauline does. Zoey apparently predicted the exact date on which Uncle Jigs would pass away—"

"A lucky guess," Stephen interjected.

"I know that. But it was enough to convince Pauline that the woman had some sort of power, and she became devoted to her."

Stephen scowled.

"I tried to discourage her at first, but whenever she visited Madame Zoey, she would come home in a much more cheerful mood. She was so distraught over losing Jigs those first few months, and I didn't see the harm in letting her spend thirty or forty dollars every week or so if it made her feel better. That's not exactly a fortune, either. She spends more than that at the beauty shop."

"But it wasn't just thirty or forty dollars, it was thousands. Look at this!" He sifted through the checks. "May tenth, three thousand dollars. May twenty-seventh, forty-five hundred. June sixteenth—five thousand!"

The staggering amounts of money were sobering enough, but the implications were worse. Jill eased one of the dining room chairs back from the table and sank into it before her weak-kneed legs dumped her on the floor. "Could they be forgeries?" she suggested hopefully.

Stephen shook his head. "I don't think so. Deposits were made from her investment fund to cover the checks, so Pauline had to have known about them."

"Then Madame Zoey somehow convinced her to pay her that money. Is that what happened?"

"Looks that way."

Jill nodded thoughtfully. This conclusion was more appealing than another one—that Pauline, in a confused state of mind, had written out the checks without realizing it. Discovering that Pauline was incompetent would be the harshest blow. At least there appeared to be a conscious intent on her aunt's part to pay Madame Zoey these obscene amounts.

"Then she must have known all along what you would find when you started digging around," Jill said.

"Which is why she's hiding out. She knew that when I discovered these checks she was going to have some explaining to do."

"Oh, Stephen, don't be too hard on her. I'm sure she realizes how gullible she's been and has learned her lesson. If you can just sort of...straighten all this out and get her back on the right track—"

"There may be nothing left to straighten out," Stephen said, his expression grim.

"Oh." The single word came out in a frightened sob.

Stephen suddenly exploded. "Of all the harebrained things! How could anyone be duped by that mumbo-jumbo?"

"Oh, Madame Zoey is very convincing. She even had me believing some of the stuff she said. She's almost...*hypnotic,* I guess is the word."

"You've been to see her?"

A knot of uncertainty formed in Jill's stomach. She hadn't actually intended to confess her visit with the psychic. "I went once with Auntie, more than a year ago, I'd say. The woman does a little of everything—crystal ball, Tarot cards, tea leaves, palms. Oh, and she channels."

"Channels? What's that?"

"She allows the spirits of the dead to speak through her. Supposedly." Jill added at Stephen's dubious look. "But she charges more for that little feat, so I didn't get to see a demonstration."

"How much more?" he asked quickly.

Jill shrugged, but she was remembering the discussion she'd had with Pauline just yesterday, regarding the spirit of Errol Flynn. Obviously her aunt wasn't a stranger to the channeling process.

"Maybe we can recover the money, or some of it," Stephen said, thinking aloud. "Now that we know who has it."

"Hey, that's a great idea," Jill said with returning optimism. "Should we call the police?" She was already moving toward the phone.

"Whoa, wait a minute. We can't do anything until we have the whole story put together, and we can't do that till Aunt Pauline gets home."

Jill returned reluctantly to her chair. "All right. What can I do to help?"

He started to hand her a stack of unopened bank statements, then hesitated. "I thought you were busy running your business," he said, carefully neutral.

"I am," she replied, thinking of all the work piling up. "But the phone orders are tapering off today. I'll catch up. Anyway, this is important." And besides, she added silently, the idea of working side by side with Stephen had a certain appeal. As a child she had categorized him as a nuisance and a wet blanket, unworthy of her attention. But now she could appreciate his orderly, logical thinking—the precision that entered into everything he did—and even envy it a bit. She herself was about as logical as Bullwinkle the Moose and as precise as a cloud.

"All right," Stephen said. "It would be useful if you could go through the rest of these statements and pick out any checks to Ryzinski. I'm going to eat my lunch." With that he picked up the white bag and went into the kitchen.

So much for working side by side with him, Jill chided herself. Was she nuts to try to befriend him, when he didn't seem inclined to reciprocate? Still, she knew she would keep trying. The more she saw of him, the more compelled she felt to unravel his mysterious mind—to find out what made him tick.

There had to be more to him than numbers and logic and a neat appearance, she thought as she thumbed through the first stack of checks. In fact, she sensed something warm and lively, shimmering just below his controlled surface. She'd caught a glimpse of it last night, when he'd talked about that ugly, unlovable cat.

She pulled out two checks to Madame Zoey from the first statement and moved on to the second, looking up from time to time to observe Stephen through the open doorway. He sat at the kitchen table, methodically eating his sandwich, stopping every few bites to take a drink from a large glass of milk. Then he would dab at his mouth with his napkin and continue. But every so often he would pause, close his eyes and take a deep breath, letting a contented smile overtake his face.

He might not dive into a meal the way she did, but he definitely was enjoying that sandwich to the fullest. This surprisingly sensual streak in him brought a strange fullness to Jill's chest, and her desire to learn more about him intensified.

The next two statements yielded nothing of interest, but the last one grabbed Jill's undivided attention. In it were three checks, dated only a couple of days apart. Each was made out to D. Z. Ryzinski—in the sum of fifty thousand dollars.

"Oh, Auntie," Jill murmured. Unless Pauline had a humdinger of an excuse, these checks amounted to pretty hard evidence that the elderly woman had slipped a cog.

Chapter Three

The smoked-turkey sandwich, which had tasted so good going down, now sat like a rock in Stephen's stomach. Although it had been two years since he'd been hospitalized for the ulcer, it still troubled him, especially when he was upset. And there could be nothing more upsetting than the sight of the three checks Jill had just shown him—unless it was the mournful expression on Jill's face.

"Oh, Stephen, what are we going to do?" she asked him. "How are we going to confront her about this?"

Stephen paced circles in the pink and aqua kitchen. "Well, first we'll ask for an explanation."

"That's only fair, I suppose," Jill agreed glumly, pacing circles in the opposite direction. "But there's no way on earth she can rationalize this."

"I'm afraid not. We're going to have to face the fact that she's no longer competent to manage her own affairs. Someone will have to take over for her. I don't suppose you..." He didn't verbalize the rest. Of all the people the court could appoint as a guardian or trustee, Jill Ballantine seemed the least likely. The judge would take one look at that wild cinnamon hair and have his doubts.

"I'd do anything to help Auntie," Jill said, "anything but manage her money. I can't even balance my own checkbook."

"We can settle that later. Right now we'd better think up a way to break the news to Pauline. Unless I miss my guess, that's the sound of her Cadillac coming up the driveway."

They both froze, listening. Moments later, Pauline bustled into the kitchen, a whirlwind dressed all in fuchsia and laden with shopping bags.

"Good morning, good morning," she called out cheerfully, as if she hadn't a care in the world. "Goodness, I suppose it's afternoon, now. I've been shopping, chickadees, and I haven't forgotten my favorite niece and nephew. For you, Jilly Bean—" She pulled a thick, hardbound book from one of her bags. "A new cookbook. It's by that chef on television, the one who visits all those exotic places."

"And for you, Stevie—" She reached into another bag and extracted a huge, fluffy beach towel emblazoned with the image of a giant calculator. "You simply have to spend some time at the beach while you're here, and I thought you might want a towel that suited your personality—I mean, your profession. You know.

"And for me—" She set a round box on the kitchen table and opened it to reveal a smart-looking pink fedora, festooned with a green feather. She plopped it on her head at a saucy angle and struck a pose. "What do you think?"

Jill and Stephen stared first at her, then at each other, speechless. Stephen was the first to recover his voice.

"Dare I ask how you paid for this stuff?"

"With credit cards, of course. I'm not in trouble with them. At least they haven't been dunning me."

"And how do you intend to pay the bill?"

She waved away his concern with forced bravado. "Oh, by the time the bill arrives, I'm sure you'll have everything straightened out. What's for lunch, Jilly?"

"A...um...chicken salad sandwich, from Jasper's," Jill mumbled as she moved toward the aqua refrigerator. "I'll get it."

"Let's not change the subject," Stephen continued. "The point is there's not much left to straighten out. I talked to your Mr. Kingston at the bank. He says the investment fund is gone. You have no more income."

Pauline stood very still for a moment, suspended in time, then wilted like a bright hibiscus bloom plucked from its life source and left too long in the sun. "It can't be that bad," she said as she sank into one of the kitchen chairs, her voice barely above a whisper. "I know I spent quite a bit of it, but not all of it. I stopped before—" Her eyes misted over and she stared down into her lap, where her thin, blue-veined hands worried the fuchsia cotton of her skirt.

Jill set a plate down on the Formica table, but her eyes were on Stephen—disapproving, accusing. She would never be able to hide anything behind those frank blue eyes.

He hadn't meant to upset Pauline, but she had to face what she'd done and admit it. That was the first step toward an ultimate solution, whatever that might be.

"Why don't you eat some lunch, Auntie," Jill said gently. "Then we'll all sit down and work this out."

Pauline nibbled at the sandwich as her worried gaze darted from Stephen to Jill and back again. They made half-hearted attempts at conversation, but eventually fell silent. An electric clock on the wall hummed away the minutes.

Finally Pauline pushed her plate away. "That's enough. I know the two of you are waiting for some type of explanation as to what I did with all that money. I'm afraid I don't really have one, not one that would satisfy you, anyway."

"We know where it went," Jill said softly. "Do you?"

"Of course. A good deal of it went to Madame Zoey. I'm sure that sounds silly to you, but she is phenomenal, truly."

"If you knew what happened to the money, why didn't you just tell me?" Stephen asked. "We could have saved a lot of time."

"Because I knew you'd think I was, well, crazy for spending so much on something you think is frivolous, and I was hoping you wouldn't find out. I thought maybe you'd just...consolidate my assets, or whatever it is accountants do for people having money problems, and you'd never really know or care how I spent the money."

"Of course we care," Jill piped in. "And we're going to get that money back, aren't we, Stephen?"

He could have wrung her pretty neck for making such a claim. "There's a slim chance," he clarified. "First I'll need to know the whole story—from the beginning." He stepped into the dining room to get his legal pad.

When he returned, Pauline appeared to be pulling herself together. She sat with her ankles crossed and her hands folded primly in her lap and launched into her story in a purposeful, seemingly sane manner.

"I used to visit Madame Zoey once a month or so, even before Jigs died," she said. "It was just something to do. I've always been fascinated with the occult, but I wasn't sure I believed in it."

Stephen nodded, remembering Pauline's Ouija board from years ago. She and Jill and some of the other cousins had entertained themselves for hours with the device, though Stephen had dismissed it as nonsense.

"When Zoey predicted the exact day Jigs would die, though, I was sold. She told me to come back after the funeral, and she would help me to guide Jigs smoothly into the afterlife. And I did. That's when she started asking for more money."

Stephen had to bite his lip to control his irritation. Madame Zoey must have no conscience, to prey on the grief of an old woman.

"It wasn't much at first, and I didn't mind paying it," Pauline continued. "It seemed a small price for staying in contact with dear Jigs. He would speak through her, you see."

"How did you know it was Jigs?" Stephen asked, careful to screen the censure out of his voice. Just the same, Jill shot him another accusing look.

"The things he would say. Little secrets only he and I knew about. And once, when he was speaking through her, I could smell his after-shave. Oh, it was him, all right." She nodded for emphasis, and her blond curls bobbed up and down.

Madame Zoey probably had been merely repeating bits of information she'd picked up over the months from Pauline herself, Stephen thought. And the after-shave was nothing more than a parlor trick. But it would be pointless to argue about it now.

"Then the trouble started," Pauline went on. "Jigs was having difficulties. He couldn't pass on to the next plane because, well, because he loved me, and he didn't want to leave me. Strong forces were trying to pull him forward, and he was digging his heels in, trying to stay here where he didn't belong. It was tearing his soul right in two."

Stephen crossed his arms and leaned back in his chair. "And I'm sure Madame Zoey knew just how to remedy the situation."

"Oh, she knew everything!" Pauline said, entirely missing his sarcasm. "But the process of sending Jigs on without harming him was a delicate operation, and one that took just loads of time and energy. Well, I couldn't expect her to do it for free, now, could I?"

Stephen made no comment.

"Anyway, once or twice a month I'd call Mr. Kingston at the bank and ask him to put more money in my checking account. After I did this a few times, he warned me that I was... how did he put it? Shaving away my principal, which I never did understand. But then I'd ask how much money I had left, and he'd say, you know, two hundred thousand, a hundred and seventy-five thousand, and so on. And it just sounded like a lot of money, so I didn't worry about it."

Obviously, Stephen wanted to say, but he refrained. He did exchange glances with Jill, though, and the raw pain he saw in her face made his heart lurch. She was hurting for her aunt. Jill did care for the older woman, he couldn't deny that, and he found himself wanting to comfort her. The thought surprised him.

"Anyway," Pauline continued, "one day Madame Zoey asked for ten thousand dollars. And that was too much. It had to stop somewhere. How much assistance does one soul need to make it to the proper plane? I mean, Jigs wasn't stupid. Surely he could have figured it out by now. So I said no. Anyway, by communicating with him through Madame Zoey I was bound to be making it worse. So I said, 'Goodbye, Jigs, good luck, you're on your own.' You don't think that was too heartless of me, do you?"

Stephen and Jill both shook their heads uncertainly. They waited for her to continue, but she merely looked around the room, avoiding their gazes, like a child expecting to be scolded.

"And then?" Stephen prompted.

"That's it! Well, I went to see her a couple of times after that, just for a Tarot card reading, and maybe a glimpse of Errol Flynn or Clark Gable, but she was very cold toward me. Except for that one little bit of information she gave me about Jill and the Virgo man, she wasn't any help at all. Last time I called to make an appointment, her number had been disconnected."

"Jill and the *what?*" Stephen asked.

"Never mind," Jill said hastily. "Auntie, when was the last time you saw Madame Zoey? Approximately."

"I can tell you exactly," Pauline said as she opened her straw handbag and extracted a pair of half glasses and a pink leather date book. She settled the glasses onto the end of her nose and thumbed through the book, pursing her lips. "September twenty-first."

"That was more than two months ago" Jill said. "Stephen, those checks—"

They both jumped up and hurried to the dining room, where the largest checks still lay on the table.

"These are dated only three weeks ago."

"What are you two talking about?" asked Pauline, who had come up behind them.

"These checks," Jill said excitedly, turning to show them to Pauline. "Did you write them?"

Pauline peered at the documents through her half glasses for several moments. Then her eyes widened and she looked up, bewildered. "I never wrote these. It looks like my handwriting, but—fifty thousand dollars? Apiece? Jigs always said I was a bit extravagant, and I'll admit that, but I'm not completely loony. Not that what I did was entirely sensible, from a certain point of view, but I knew my limits. I wouldn't deliberately kill the goose that lays the golden eggs—or in this case, wipe out the nest egg that Jigs left for me."

Jill suddenly threw her arms around Pauline's neck and hugged her. "Oh, Auntie, thank goodness!"

"Then you *did* think I was crazy," Pauline said, gently disengaging herself from Jill's enthusiastic embrace. "I guess I can't blame you." She frowned. "Did Madame Zoey steal that money from me?"

"Looks that way," Stephen replied. "She must have taken some blank checks out of your purse—did you even know any were missing?"

"Well, no." Pauline said, her voice filled with apology, "but since I never remember to write them down in one of those thingamajigs—"

"A register?" Jill supplied.

"Right. I probably wouldn't have noticed. But how did that much money get into my checking account in the first place?"

"My guess is she impersonated you," Stephen said, "and instructed the bank to liquidate your investments."

"She could have gotten Mr. Kingston's name and phone number from your address book," Jill added.

"But there was a secret code!" Pauline objected. "Even Mr. Kingston, who knew my voice, always asked for my mother's maiden name and a secret number... which I wrote down by his phone number in my address book. I guess that wasn't very smart, was it."

"I'd have done the same thing," Jill said in a vain effort to comfort her aunt.

Pauline shook her head sadly. "I can't believe Madame Zoey would stoop to such a thing."

"Aunt Pauline, that's her business," Stephen said. "She's a professional con artist. Now are you convinced she's a phony?"

Pauline looked affronted at the suggestion. "Of course not. She has a gift. She could be a crook and still have a gift, couldn't she? If you'd heard some of the amazing things—"

"Never mind that," Stephen said, effectively cutting off his aunt. "I'm going to call Kingston and get his side of the story. Then we'll go to the police."

"Oh, my, the police?" Pauline paled visibly. "I think I'll just go take a nap."

"You do that," Stephen said, feeling like he could get more done without having to worry about the elderly woman's sensibilities. "Just promise me one thing. You don't leave here without telling us where you're going. And don't spend any more money, not even with plastic. Think of yourself as temporarily bankrupt."

"Yes, of course," she answered distractedly as she wandered toward her bedroom.

When Pauline was gone, Jill turned on him. "Did you have to say that? Did you have to use the word *bankrupt?*"

"Why not? It's true!"

"But you upset her. And it's not her fault. She was duped. Anyone can be taken in by a good con artist, and Madame Zoey was good."

"Who are you to judge that?" Stephen said, smiling despite the current situation's gravity. "You're not exactly a skeptic yourself. I seem to remember a certain little redheaded girl who got taken in by the shell game?"

"I was only ten when that happened," she said hotly. Stephen was referring to an incident when a smooth operator had cornered her at the beach and coaxed her into guessing which shell hid the pea. She'd been so positive she could outwit the con man, and had ended up losing two weeks' allowance.

"That guy was so sloppy with his sleight of hand, a three year old could have spotted the trick," Stephen said. "If I hadn't come along—"

"Yes, and you rubbed it in for days afterward. Let's get back to business, shall we? You were going to call Mr. Kingston."

"Right." He made a conscious effort to recapture a more sober mood. What had overcome him, teasing Jill when there were serious matters to deal with? Then again, she was eminently teasable. She was ticklish, he remembered, on the bottoms of her feet, behind her knees and under her arms. If he tickled her now, would she shriek with laughter the way she had as a little girl?

No, she'd probably slug him, he decided. He wanted to see her smile again, but he wasn't willing to risk a fat lip for the privilege.

"So what's this about you and a Virgo man?" Stephen brought up the subject abruptly the following day as he and Jill, riding in her army-surplus jeep, careered toward the Del Rosa police station.

His question so flustered her that she failed to avoid one of the many potholes gracing the resort town's narrow streets, resulting in a bone-rattling bump. She had hoped that Pauline's reference to the Virgo man would be overlooked, but apparently not.

"Oh, it was nothing," she said. But seeing the intensely curious look in Stephen's penetrating gray eyes, she knew she wouldn't get away with evasiveness. She stopped for a light and turned her full attention on him. He had one of those haircuts that, even after the wind blew it in a hundred different directions, it fell right back into place.

"If it was nothing, why don't you tell me about it?" he asked.

"It's nonsense, really. Madame Zoey said I should be on my guard, that a Virgo man would cause me great pain and sorrow."

"I see." The smile faded, and he looked vaguely disappointed. "I'm a Virgo."

"Yes, I know." She'd been hoping perhaps he *didn't* know.

"Then are you on your guard against me?"

"I didn't need Madame Zoey to warn me about you. I would have been on my guard no matter what." She didn't put much bite into the quip.

The light turned green and she stamped down on the accelerator as she realized something: she didn't dislike Stephen anymore. In fact, he fascinated her. He was so very different from her, and yet it was that contrast that drew her. She wanted to get closer, if for no other reason than to learn something about human nature that she couldn't learn from herself.

He was still recognizable as the Stevie Whitfield who had plagued her otherwise-carefree stays with Aunt Pauline, but ten years had softened the hard edges. The superior posturing had been replaced by a more quiet confidence, and she couldn't ignore the way he had selflessly devoted his vacation to bail out his aunt.

Yes, she was definitely starting to like and respect him. And the more she liked him, the easier it would be for him to hurt her. She could take criticism from any number of strangers, and the barbs would bounce right off her thick skin, leaving her unscathed. Only the people she was close to, those she liked and respected, had the power to hurt her.

Maybe Madame Zoey hadn't been so far off the mark.

Their arrival at the old stone police station ended Jill's speculation. She couldn't afford the luxury of playing "What if" with Stephen. She had a more immediate objective—to get Pauline's money back.

She wasn't thrilled when Detective Lamont Herschel was assigned to hear their complaint. Although she was only slightly acquainted with him—his wife played cards with Pauline—she knew that he was slow, plodding and methodical. She would have much preferred dealing with a more energetic go-getter. It was going to take a smart cookie to outwit the conniving Madame Zoey.

They gave Herschel all the information they had—all the checks, Madame Zoey's last known address, her description. They put him in touch with Mr.

Kingston, who earlier had confirmed their theory about Zoey impersonating Pauline over the phone. Apparently she'd said all the right things, given the proper codes, because the transaction had caused barely a raised eyebrow.

"I'll get with the Santa Monica police and the LAPD, see what they can turn up on this D. Z. Ryzinski," Herschel said, smoothing his sparse black hair over his balding head in a habitual gesture. "I'm awfully sorry to see this happen to Pauline," he added. "If there's anything Lizzy or me can do, on a personal basis, you'll let me know, won't you?"

Jill felt uncomfortable at his concern. Perhaps she still retained a smidgen of her proper Boston upbringing, because she hated airing family problems to an outsider, especially when those problems engendered pity. "Yes, I will," she murmured as she and Stephen rose to leave.

"He seemed like a sensible, intelligent sort," Stephen commented as they climbed into the lemon-yellow jeep.

"Sensible, intelligent and slow as a slug," Jill replied. She sighed hopelessly. "I'm afraid Auntie will never see that money again."

"Probably not," Stephen agreed. "Which is all the more reason for us to contain her spending habits. It's not that she's actually bankrupt. In going through her papers I've discovered some assets—bonds, CDs. But most of it can't be liquidated at this point. Of course there's the house—"

Jill gasped. "You wouldn't think of selling her house, would you?" she asked, appalled at the very idea.

"No, of course not. She does own her home outright, and we could take out a mortgage on it if things get desperate. But I was actually talking about her little beach cottage. As I recall it's not much, but—"

"Not much!" Jill repeated indignantly, picturing the tiny bungalow on stilts, perched on a stretch of sand just a few miles south of Del Rosa. "Better not let Pauline hear you say that. She loves that place." And Jill did, too, for that matter. She'd spent many a summer day playing there, spinning fantasies of pirates and buried treasure at the beach. If it rained she would play on the balcony, imagining herself a captive princess waiting to be rescued from the tower by the handsome prince. When she was older she'd thrown beach parties at the house with her friends, and more recently she'd spent quiet days there when she needed to get away from the clamor of ringing phones and chirping birds.

"Well, I mean it's a small house," Stephen clarified. "But it's on the beach, and even with my limited knowledge of California real estate, I know that translates into bundles of money. If she puts it on the market immediately, asks a reasonable price for it, I'm sure it would sell quickly—"

Jill slammed on the brakes, stopping the jeep in the middle of a block. "No."

"What do you mean, 'No'?"

"I mean *no*. You can't sell the beach cottage. It means too much to her."

"Having money to live on means a lot to her, too," Stephen pointed out. "Besides, she's not using it."

"She visited there just last month," Jill argued. "In fact, she's gone there a lot since Jigs died. It's where they lived when they were first married, before Jigs got rich in Silicon Valley."

"I can appreciate that," Stephen said patiently. "But I have to act in Pauline's best interest. I'll recommend that she sell the beach house. Ultimately the decision will be up to her, anyway. Can we go now?"

The jeep was still stopped in the middle of the block. Reluctantly Jill put it into gear and accelerated. "You know she'll do whatever you tell her to do. She's ashamed that she allowed Madame Zoey to take her for a ride, and she'll do whatever she thinks she has to in order to redeem herself." Jill stopped the jeep again. "Stephen, don't make her sell the beach cottage."

"I won't make her do anything she doesn't want to do," he insisted. But his face was hard, implacable.

And Jill had actually believed that she was starting to like him! With a disgusted snort she started the jeep moving. But they'd scarcely gone more than a few feet when inspiration struck and she braked again.

"I've got it! Why not rent out the house to vacationers? Beachfront houses are in demand year-round, so Pauline would be assured of a steady income."

"You want Pauline to be a property manager?" Stephen asked dubiously.

"No, we'll get an agent to find the renters and handle the money. It's done all the time." She could see Stephen was considering her suggestion. The inflexibility in his expression had softened a bit. She pressed her advantage. "It's a good idea, Stephen. She can rent it out just until she doesn't need the money anymore and then she'll still own the place."

Jill put a pleading hand on his forearm, surprised to find it hard as concrete beneath the starched cotton of his sleeve. Weren't accountants supposed to be sedentary? How did he keep in shape? she wondered. It felt surprisingly pleasant to touch him. The fabric beneath her palm was warm from the sun.

"Maybe," he said, jarring her from her sensual wanderings.

"What?"

"Maybe," he said again, staring at her as if she were daft. Then he looked down at the hand on his arm.

She pulled away self-consciously.

"I'll have to take a look at it first," he continued sensibly, "see what condition it's in. Has it been improved significantly in the past few years? The last time I saw it, it was pretty shabby looking."

"Well...actually it hasn't," Jill admitted. But she couldn't recall if it just needed a bit of paint, or major repairs. In truth, she always looked past the obvious when she went there. It was the mood of the place that mattered to her, a welcoming feeling of warmth and wellbeing, of happy memories and lots of love.

If only she could make Stephen see it as she did, he wouldn't think of selling it. *That's it.* Abruptly she accelerated again, and pulled a U-turn in the middle of the intersection.

"What the hell are you doing?" Stephen demanded as he grabbed on to the door handle with one hand and the edge of his seat with another, holding on for dear life.

"We're going to see the beach cottage," she answered breezily, heading for I-5.

"Now?" he protested.

"Sure, why not? No sense putting it off, and anyway, it's not a long drive. You even said you wanted me to take you to the beach during your visit, show you around. I'm showing you around."

"But I have things to do. I have to check in at my office. My partner called this morning when I was in the shower, and I haven't gotten back to him yet. Then I need to fix that screen door so the damn cat will stay put..." He gave up when he saw that Jill wasn't listening. Full of purpose, she was on a one-track course for Pauline's beach house, and nothing he could say would stop her—which in some ways was a good thing. They hadn't been getting very far, what with her slamming on the brakes every few seconds.

"Do you always do everything on impulse?" he asked.

She nodded, then flashed a defiant smile at him. "It works for me. If I sit and try to puzzle things out, or make elaborate plans, I never get anything done."

That made sense, he supposed. But it wouldn't work for him. If he followed even half of his impulses, he'd get himself in trouble. Like right now. He had an impulse to touch that wildly blowing cinnamon hair, to bury his face in it and immerse himself in the fragrance that he only caught a whiff of now and then. He had an impulse to taste—

He gripped his knees with his hands and kept his eyes focused on the road ahead of them until the Jeep's tires crunched onto the beach house's shell driveway.

He found it hard to concentrate on the house with his mind still inexorably, inappropriately straying to Jill. She looked soft and summery in a billowy skirt of bleached denim and an apricot-colored cotton sweater. She was like cool morning sunlight, and all he could think about was capturing a piece of it for himself.

Even before today he'd experienced some funny feelings about Jill—a tightening in his chest when she ventured too near, a fleeting curiosity, barely acknowledged, about the texture of her skin. Her sunny smile caused a fluttering in his stomach—he'd noticed that before. But it hadn't hit him full force until she'd touched his arm, just a few minutes ago. Her hand had felt so full of life, causing him to tingle with awareness. It was then he'd admitted that he wanted her.

"Needs a coat of paint," she said, gazing up at the sagging house.

Stephen forced his attention to the matter at hand. The house looked awful, worse than he'd anticipated, especially when compared to its stylish, smartly painted neighbors.

He and Jill walked around the perimeter, pausing to stare up at the front, which faced a beautiful view of the sea. That view, at least, hadn't deteriorated. But the house itself appeared to be staggering on its stilts.

"Do you think it's safe?" Stephen asked as Jill led him toward a flight of rickety stairs.

"It's been here fifty years," she replied, climbing the steps without hesitation. "I don't think it's going to pick now to fall down."

Stephen wasn't so sure, but he followed Jill, anyway, fascinated with the upward progress of her dainty feet, clad in apricot espadrilles. As the full skirt swirled behind her, he caught a glimpse of the backs of her knees. She had quite a pair of legs on her, no doubt about that. And why the hell he couldn't stop thinking about them was a mystery. Why was she suddenly so...so sexy?

The front porch creaked as they walked across it. Some of the planking would need to be replaced if Pauline were to rent the place out.

Jill found the key hidden on top of a window frame and opened the front door, allowing them entrance to the stuffy interior.

The inside was worse than the outside, Stephen observed with a frown. Not only did everything need repainting, but the furniture was in poor repair and hopelessly outdated. The wiring would need some attention, he thought when he noticed the old-fashioned fixtures. The kitchen appliances were forty years old if they were a day, and the plumbing shrieked in protest when he turned on the kitchen tap.

"See? Everything works," Jill said when Stephen tested the bathroom faucets. She stood less than a foot behind him in the small room, until he found it difficult to take an even breath. He imagined her touching his back, sliding her hands around his ribcage, pressing herself against him...

"Damn," he muttered as he turned abruptly and strode out of the closeness of that room, nearly pushing her off balance in his hurry to get through the door.

"It's not that bad," she called after him, misunderstanding his reaction. "Some cleaning, a little paint, maybe a few throw rugs, new curtains, slipcovers for the furniture..."

He entered the last remaining room, the master bedroom, Jill right behind. An antique iron bed covered by a bright quilt dominated the room, and Jill wasted no time rushing to it and jumping onto the bouncy mattress.

"Isn't this a great bed?" she asked him, still on her sales pitch. "I've always loved it. You should try it out."

Not on your life! He almost said it aloud. His traitorous imagination had taken liberties with the fetching picture Jill made, stretched out across the bed. The thought of her naked against cool sheets almost did him in.

What the hell was wrong with him? He'd never had a problem concentrating on business matters, no matter what distractions beckoned him. What was more, he didn't even *like* Jill, never had and never would. Not that she wasn't a basically fine person, but she made him uncomfortable with her sharp tongue and her utterly incomprehensible logic. That she should provoke a physical response in him made no sense. She wasn't his type at all.

With another muttered curse he walked back through the stuffy house and outside to the front porch, where he stood against the railing and let the ocean breeze cool him down. He was thankful that Jill took her time about following him, leaving him a few moments of calming solitude.

He finally managed to pull his thoughts together. The decision on the house was easy. What to do about Jill should have been easier still. *Nothing.* She would probably laugh if she even suspected the crazy thoughts he'd been entertaining about her.

She would never know, because he would never tell her or give her any indication. He would simply turn it *off,* dammit. Keeping his baser urgings under wraps had never been a problem, and it shouldn't be one now. Just as he controlled his brief flashes of temper, he could control desire.

He turned, full of purpose, intending to tell Jill of his decision about the house and firmly insist that they return home immediately. But she was right there, having just come up behind him, and he did knock her off balance this time.

They both took a step backward and mumbled automatically, "Sorry."

"Stephen, you haven't said two words since we got here. What do you think? We could whip it into shape without much trouble, couldn't we? I'd be willing to do the work, and I'm sure Pauline would help."

She looked so hopeful, he really hated to disappoint her. But the bottom line was what mattered. "It would cost a lot of money to get this place fixed up to the point we could rent it out," he said. "And I know you'd like to help, but you've got your own business to run. Besides, who's going to buy the paint, the lumber, the new furniture? No, the sensible thing is to put it on the market and sell it as is."

Her face fell, and he felt like a heel. "But Stephen, this place isn't just a hunk of real estate. It's a piece of the past, of Pauline's past and mine, too. It has a feeling that can't be captured any place else, and if you sell it, that unique atmosphere will be gone forever. Can't you feel it? Can't you feel how special it is?"

He almost could, especially when she took both his hands in hers and stared up at him with those luminous blue eyes. Her face was so close he could count the freckles on her nose and feel the warmth of her breath.

Later he never knew how it happened. But all of a sudden she was in his arms.

Chapter Four

Jill didn't bother to analyze how it had happened or why. All she knew was that Stephen was kissing her like she'd never been kissed in her life, and nothing had ever felt this wonderful.

His mouth was hard, yet oddly gentle on hers; his arms held her firmly, insistently, but with a certain unmistakable reverence. Every cell in her body vibrated with the sudden, inexplicable need to share herself with him—not just physically, but emotionally, too, and she didn't for a moment question that need.

The kiss deepened, became harder, more demanding, heating her blood, eroding her control. She tunneled her fingers through his thick, dark hair, enjoying its silky texture. In fact, she couldn't get enough of the feel of him, the rough and the smooth of him. She pressed her hips wantonly against his, and the contact sent a thrill shimmering up her spine and down her legs.

With a hoarse moan he broke the kiss and buried his face in her hair.

"You see, this place is magic," she whispered near his ear. "We can't sell it. Oh, Stephen, please tell me we don't have to sell it."

He grasped her shoulders and slowly pushed her away from him, until he could look her in the eyes. "That magic comes from you, Cinnamon Girl, not the house."

His voice was deliciously husky, and in those changeable gray eyes, for once open and full of wonder, she saw the promise of warmth and laughter and thousands of kisses just like the first one.

But before she could respond to that promise, something changed. Like a window shade slowly lowering to hide the contents of a warm, inviting home, his expression gradually closed, and his eyes hardened to the color of flint.

"What's wrong?" she asked, scared of his answer.

"Nothing," he responded quickly, too quickly. He set her firmly apart from him and turned away, to stare out at the endless sea. "Nothing except I went temporarily insane. Sorry. It won't happen again."

She was stunned, utterly flabbergasted, by his abrupt change of mood. "How can you kiss me like that and then dismiss it as a moment of insanity?" she demanded.

"You're very pretty, Jill," he said, in an emotionless tone that belied the words. He wouldn't look at her. "When a woman as attractive as you offers herself to a man the way you just did, she should expect to get a response. But I'm not interested. I'm here to do a job and then go home."

"*Offers herself?*" she repeated, horrified. "I did no such thing. You started it."

"It doesn't matter who started it. I'm ending it," he said with a note of finality. The discussion was closed.

"Fine." She swept her way off the porch and down the stairs, swallowing back tears of shock and frustration. Maybe she carried her feelings much too close to the surface, but she was now convinced that Stephen didn't *have* any feelings. Anyone who could say such cold, hateful things...

But she couldn't forget those few moments when he had, perhaps accidentally, let her experience the warmth that was captured in his soul. She'd made him feel something, all right. So he wasn't devoid of emotion. He just didn't want anyone to know it was there—especially her.

By the time he joined her in the jeep, his face and body language carefully neutral, her anger had ebbed considerably. Maybe she should try a different approach, something less threatening. If she let him know how she honestly felt about this whole thing, maybe he would open up, too.

"Are we going to sit here all day?" he snapped. "Or are you going to start the engine?"

"In a minute." She turned toward him and touched his shoulder. He actually flinched, and his body stiffened until he was rigid as a tree trunk. Still, she pressed on. "Stephen, there's nothing wrong with what happened back there. In fact, I...I rather enjoyed it." The words tumbled out. "And I'd be open to doing it again some time. A lot's changed since we were kids, huh?"

She was getting nowhere fast. If anything, Stephen appeared even more closed to her than he had moments ago. He'd twisted around in his seat until he virtually had his back turned to her.

She pulled her hand away and started the jeep, angry that she'd let him sting her again. So much for sharing honest feelings.

Less than an hour ago she'd told Stephen that she seldom stopped to puzzle things out or make elaborate plans. But this was a special case. She would have to give some more thought as to how best to deal with him. She did know one thing—she wasn't about to dismiss what had just happened. The possibilities were too intriguing.

They exchanged not a word during the drive home. As soon as Jill screeched to a stop in the carport, Stephen hopped out and went quickly inside the house.

It was obvious to Jill he was in a helluva hurry to get away from her. She shook her head as she went inside her own quarters. Good thing she enjoyed a challenge.

She spent the rest of the afternoon filling orders for Spice Up Your Life. She was falling further behind, and the phone calls were still pouring in. At one point she realized she'd gotten some of the prepaid orders mixed up with the to-be-billed ones, and she had to backtrack, repacking several boxes and negating at least two hours of work.

She just couldn't seem to concentrate. Her mind kept wandering back to the fiery kiss at the beach. Even now her memory was still reconstructing little bits of the experience—how the salt breeze had teased her hair and billowed under her skirt in a vain attempt to cool her, and the intriguing smell of Stephen's after-shave. The scent had offered an odd contrast to their surroundings, reminded her of autumn and falling leaves, wood smoke and the promise of snow—and home, the home back East she sometimes still missed.

After the UPS man came and went, taking with him a load of completed orders, she quit for the day. There were a couple of recipes she wanted to try from the new cookbook Pauline had given her, and this was as good a time as any.

Jill headed for the bedroom, intending to fetch the cookbook from her nightstand, where she'd left it last night after reading herself to sleep. But *Astrology for the Beginner* caught her eye, and all thoughts of chicken Pyrenees with mushroom-currant sauce fled from her mind.

So far the astrology book had been uncannily accurate in describing Stephen's personality. Could Jill take it one step further? Could this book possibly help her to understand the undoubtedly complicated reasons behind his recent behavior? Could she come up with a new strategy using the stars as a guide?

It was worth a try. She took the book into the sun room and settled into a deck chair. There, serenaded by the comforting din of chirps from her flock of finches, she read more about the Virgo man.

The section on romance, which she'd only skimmed before, held some particularly interesting gems of wisdom.

"If you want to woo a Virgo man," the text read, "an aggressive approach won't do it. Patience is the virtue that will win his finicky affections."

Patience? Unfortunately that was one virtue Jill had never practiced. Her parents maintained that it was a common fault of her entire generation, but she did tend to expect immediate results for her efforts.

She didn't have *time* for patience. Stephen would be leaving soon. He couldn't stay away indefinitely from his accounting practice in Madison. His partner called at least twice a day to consult with Stephen about unexpected problems that had cropped up.

"A neat appearance and tidy surroundings will impress the Virgo, making him feel comfortable." Yes, she'd read that part before, Jill remembered. But neatness just wasn't one of her fortes. She looked down at herself, taking in the cutoff jeans, one leg shorter than the other, and her faded green St. Patrick's Day T-shirt. She couldn't even get the holiday right!

These *were* her work clothes, she rationalized. If she wore nice things, she'd just get them dirty. Problem was, she often dressed like this whether she was working or not. She'd made a special effort earlier today, in honor of her visit to the police station. But skirts and stylish tops were the exception, not the norm, in her wardrobe.

Without even glancing over her shoulder, she knew what her apartment looked like—empty boxes everywhere; torn newspapers, which she used for packing material, littering the floor; half-read magazines lying about; wilting house plants, which she always forgot to water. Nutmeg would be spilled on everything after her earlier frenzy of order filling.

It wasn't that she didn't maintain a certain degree of cleanliness, per the health department's rules. But that didn't stop her from cluttering up the place.

It was a hopeless case, she concluded with a sigh. If Stephen had experienced a moment of lust, it must have been temporary insanity, just as he'd alleged. Here was a man who no doubt folded his underwear, shopped for groceries with a list and arranged his bookcase alphabetically. He would never consciously get mixed up with a woman who stuffed clothes into drawers willy-nilly, purchased groceries on impulse and stacked her books vertically with no discernible order. She would drive him stark-raving loony.

"Well, that's that," she said aloud as she resolutely set the astrology book aside and picked up the cookbook. But no matter how hard she tried to concentrate on her recipes, her thoughts kept straying back in forbidden directions, reliving memories that were best forgotten, touching on future events that would never take place.

Stephen sat at his aunt's dining room table and scanned the papers he'd received a few minutes ago. He'd spent most of the afternoon with a real estate agent and was very satisfied with the results.

Although Pauline had at first resisted his suggestion about selling the beach cottage, she had soon come around to his way of thinking. It was the only solution that made sense. And when the agent had recommended an astronomical asking price, even with the house in such poor condition, Stephen was elated. If it sold for anywhere near that amount, the money would go a long way toward restoring Pauline's nest egg.

Now if only Jill would stay out of it. With that cursed romanticism of hers, he was afraid she would change Pauline's mind.

Jill. That afternoon he'd kept himself so busy that he'd managed to avoid thoughts of her. But now that his work for the day was finished, he couldn't help but recall the exchange they'd shared earlier.

Exchange. That was a cold way of putting it. It was a kiss, for heaven's sake, and a damn nice one. He'd thoroughly enjoyed it, up to a point. Pressed up against him, she felt even better than she looked, all soft and womanly, vibrating with an energy all her own.

The kiss itself hadn't rattled him nearly as much as it should have. No, it was the stuff that came after the kiss, when he'd looked into her eyes and realized that she'd touched a softer, more tender part of him he hadn't even known existed. For one insane moment he had actually considered giving in to her plea not to sell the beach house, for no more reason than sentimentality.

Such behavior just didn't make sense. In the business world he had earned a reputation as a cool, calculating decision maker. Not that he was ruthless. But he could take a company in financial trouble and as cleanly as a surgeon with a sharp scalpel, cut out whatever was causing the loss. It might be a product or service, an overpaid, underworked executive—sometimes even a whole department. Whatever wasn't carrying its own weight had to go, and ultimately the business profited.

There was no reason the same tactics shouldn't work for his aunt's situation. Emotion had no business rearing its ugly head where money was concerned. And yet he'd almost let that happen. *That* was scary, scary enough to make him back off, way off, from Jill and everything she represented. She muddled his thinking, and he couldn't afford that. Pauline needed him in top form.

Still, he knew he hadn't been nice or fair to Jill. She hadn't deserved that cold shoulder or his nastiness. He would have to make it up to her, preferably in some safe, impersonal way. He could start by apologizing, he supposed.

He stacked the papers neatly, ready for Pauline's signature. Then he stood, turned and headed into the kitchen, intending to seek Jill out and put things right between them. He hated leaving untidy edges around a relationship, any relationship.

He paused with his hand on the kitchen doorknob, remembering what just the sight of her had done to him earlier that day. Was he ready to face her again?

He took a deep breath and conjured up her image in his mind. Though he had to admit the mental picture was alluring, he detected no strange tingles or tremors or waves of burgeoning passion. He concluded that whatever strange spell he'd come under earlier was gone now. His hormones were once again firmly under his control.

With a smile of satisfaction he continued out the door and across the carport, skirting Jill's yellow jeep. Why would anyone want to drive such a hideous, impractical vehicle? he wondered. But he wouldn't pose that question aloud, not if he wanted to make peace.

A mouth-watering aroma drifted through the screen door. He knocked, idly hoping that she might share whatever it was she was cooking for dinner.

"Come in," she called out in a cheerful voice.

Had he expected her to be sulking? He opened the door to let himself in, catching first a whiff, then the overpowering scent of something spicy. He started to look for Jill, but the condition of her living room stopped him cold.

Good God, did she actually *live* in this bedlam? She could have applied for national disaster relief. There was hardly a square inch of carpet showing, as it was covered with boxes, newspapers, magazines, packing tapes, address labels, pens and pencils, wilted houseplants, various stacks of mail and a large sack of birdseed.

The top of her small desk, which sat in a corner of the living room, was likewise covered. Notes were Scotch taped to drawer fronts, window shades and lamps: "Mrs. Gowing's lawn, Thursday," and "Tuesday, deliver four zebras to Mission Mall Pets." Another read, "New shrubs to arrive on the twenty-fifth."

The twenty-fifth of this month, or was that note from last year? he wondered. If it was current, that would be another bill of Pauline's to pay.

"Auntie, is that you?" Jill called out.

Guilty over his snooping, he turned toward the kitchen. She appeared in the doorway just as he waded into the dining room, and her curious expression dissolved into one of cool indifference.

"Oh, it's you," she said.

"Hi." His mouth felt suddenly dry, for the actual sight of her was decidedly more potent than his imaginary picture—even though she wore another of her shapeless T-shirts, and flour was smeared across one cheek. A faded purple apron rode low on her slender hips. She'd pulled her hair back from her face in a clip of some sort, and several tendrils had escaped to dance around her face.

"Did you need something?"

"Not exactly, it's just that—what are you cooking?"

"Chicken Pyrenees with mushroom-currant sauce. There's plenty for all three of us, so you and Pauline can join me if you like. It's such a nice evening, I thought we could dine al fresco."

"Do you cook for Pauline very often?" he asked.

"We trade back and forth. But since you won't let her buy groceries, I'm taking over for a while."

"Oh, for heaven's sake, I never told her she couldn't buy groceries."

"You told her not to buy anything, and she'll do whatever you tell her to. She's feeling very inadequate right now, so she's relying totally on your judgment. You have to be careful what you say to her."

"Look, I'll have a talk with her later, okay? I didn't come over here to discuss Pauline."

Jill looked down her nose at him. "Then why are you here?"

He ran a finger along the white plastic cloth that covered her dining room table, picking up a dab of the fine brown powder that dusted the surface—the source of the spicy aroma. "To apologize," he finally said. "I behaved very badly this afternoon. The whole thing took me off guard. I don't like surprises, and I don't always react well to them."

She raised one eyebrow, and though he didn't think his apology was at all funny, the corner of her mouth twitched in amusement.

"What part surprised you?" she asked, her voice gilded with barely contained laughter. "The fact that I 'offered myself' to you, or the fact that you accepted?"

He could feel a dull heat radiating from his face. "All right, I guess I deserved that. *'Offer yourself'* was an unfortunate choice of words. But to answer your question, the whole thing was rash and unwise on both our parts, and I hope we can put it behind us so we can continue to work together to help Pauline."

He was cute when he blushed, Jill thought. He was also unarguably right. Hadn't she, just a few minutes ago, concluded that the two of them would make a horrendous match? "Agreed," she said, forcing a smile.

"Good. When's dinner?"

"In a little while. It has to simmer a few minutes."

"Then you have time to explain what all this stuff is. Something to do with your infamous mail-order business, I presume." With a sweeping gesture he indicated the chaos of her dining and living rooms. This was the first time he'd been inside her apartment since he'd arrived two days ago, and she desperately wished he'd given her some warning so she could have straightened up.

Then again, what did it matter if he thought she was a slob?

"It's called Spice Up Your Life," she began reluctantly. "Sort of a seasoning-of-the-month club. November is nutmeg—ties in well with holiday baking and all. For the very reasonable price of fifteen ninety-five, plus three dollars shipping and handling, each customer receives the featured spice in a lead crystal decanter with an old-fashioned, hand-done calligraphy label."

She handed him one of the sparkling jars, which he examined closely, holding it up to the light.

"And," she continued with growing confidence, "you also get a history of the spice, how and where it's grown and processed and a collection of mouth-watering, kitchen-tested gourmet recipes using the featured spice."

She handed him one of her specially printed leaflets.

"And," she said in her best television huckster voice, "the next one hundred members receive, absolutely free, this handsome clear acrylic spice rack in which to beautifully display your collection of spices as it grows."

She pulled one of the spice racks from a box under the table and set it out for Stephen to see.

"If you're not completely satisfied, return the spice at our expense, but keep the rack as our gift. There's absolutely no obligation, no minimum order. Call today."

She waited, holding her breath. She'd told no one about this venture except Pauline, not even her parents. So many of her small-business ideas had flopped in the past that no one had any faith in her anymore. Even Pauline, who had financed part of Spice Up Your Life, had her doubts. Thus it was doubly important that Stephen give her some sign of approval.

He appeared interested, at least. "What's your profit margin?"

She'd been prepared for the question. "Not much on the first order, because of the spice rack. But after that, about five dollars per shipment." Or thereabouts. She wasn't really certain, but if she admitted that to Stephen he would nail her for sure.

"And people really go for this kind of thing? They pay almost twenty dollars for a spice they can get at the grocery store for two or three bucks?"

She nodded.

"How many takers have you gotten?"

"In the three months since I started, almost seven hundred."

He put a hand to his head and sank into the nearest chair. "That's thirty-five hundred dollars a month profit, and you've hardly scratched the surface. Jill, you have a potential gold mine here."

"Well, maybe," she demured. "Most of that seven hundred are new customers who responded to an ad I put in *Southern Cooking* magazine, so it hasn't paid off yet. But it will. I've had almost no returns or cancellations."

"I'm truly impressed," Stephen said.

Jill felt herself growing warm all over. He would never know how much those words of approval meant to her. But the glow was short-lived.

"Where's your computer?"

She sat down across from him, letting the table form a protective barrier between them. "I, um, don't have one."

"Then how do you keep track of your members? You're not paying an outside service to do it, are you?"

"No. I do it myself... with rubber bands," she mumbled. "I write each customer's name and address and credit card number on a piece of paper, then I stack them together and wrap the orders that need to be filled with a red rubber band and the ones still to be paid with a green one and the ones that are all caught up till next month with a blue one. The first-time orders have a separate system, of course."

"Of course," he repeated faintly, though with every word she'd spoken, he'd grown a little paler. "Could you show me?" he asked. "I thought I was familiar with every form of accounting in existence, but this I have to see."

"I'd really rather not," she said, lifting her chin a notch. "Not if you're going to make fun of it. I know it sounds like an unorthodox system, but it works for me."

He nodded, accepting her explanation for now. "What percentage of your profits do you intend to reinvest? Do you have a business plan?"

"I'm not even sure what one is," she admitted, drumming her fingers on the table.

"Projected profit and loss, a timetable for the next twelve months at least—"

"How could I know that? I'd rather just see how much money comes in. Speaking of which, Pauline owns twenty-five percent. As soon as I start making a profit she'll get her cut. That will help her situation, won't it?"

"Eventually. But you shouldn't count on a big profit for several months, at least. The key to making a small business grow is reinvesting. You might want to think about television advertising. Historically this type of scheme lends itself to TV ads. And you'll definitely want to hire an employee to help you with order fulfillment. It's clear you can't continue doing it all yourself. And of course you'll need someone to keep your books—"

"Stephen! Would you slow down, please? Look, I don't want Spice Up Your Life to become the next Ginsu Knife. I'm not interested in owning a large company. All I want is to pay my bills and have a little left over."

"But why would you settle for that when this concept you've developed could make you quite comfortable? You could at least listen to my advice. Normally I charge a substantial fee for my consulting service. And if you don't get someone to help you straighten out this mess, it's going to get out of control and strangle you."

This was too much. She shot up out of her chair, unable to contain her irritation any longer. "I am running my business just fine without your oh-so-valuable help, thank you. It might be a little messy, a little confusing from the standpoint of a controlling person like you, but I know exactly what's going on. I'm staying afloat, I'm having fun and I'm *succeeding* all by myself, so I'll thank you to keep your over-organized mitts off my spices!"

Stephen stared at her, almost awestruck by the fire in her he'd unwittingly sparked to life. Moments ago he'd been thinking what fun it would be if he could get hold of her little mail-order business and straighten it out for her. He loved taking something chaotic and illogical and turning it into a finely tuned business machine.

Now all he could think about was getting hold of the business *owner* and taking her to bed for a week—after he brushed the flour off her face and took a comb to that tangled mop she called hair.

Dammit, he was doing it again! Just when he thought his hormones were under control, he was once again fantasizing about sex with this nut case cousin-by-marriage. Casual liaisons just weren't his style. When he entered into a relationship—which hadn't happened often—he went into it logically, slowly and with plenty of thought toward the future.

His unpredictable dealings with Jill simply didn't bode well for a future. He had to get these ridiculous notions out of his head.

"Is something burning?" he asked casually. Then he couldn't resist adding, "Besides you, that is."

"Oh, the sauce." She whirled around and disappeared into the kitchen without another word.

He shook his head and headed for the door. Escape seemed the wisest course of action. But as soon as he opened it a streak of black fur bolted between his legs, making a beeline for the open French doors that led out onto Jill's sun porch.

"Boniface! What do you think you're doing?" He followed the cat as quickly as possible, but his progress was slow through the obstacle course of Jill's living room. By the time he reached the sun porch, Boniface was already perched on the highest piece of furniture and contemplating how to jump to the nearest bird cage. The tiny birds, sensing danger, were kicking up an ear-splitting fuss.

The din made him nervous. How could Jill stand that constant chirping, day after day?

Stephen grabbed the cat before any real harm was done. "Don't you know better than to pick on someone smaller than you?" he scolded as he held the animal tightly against his shoulder. "If you're so bent on feathers for dinner, why don't you go outside and catch a wild bird?"

On the way out of the room, a book sitting on a low table by a deck chair caught his eye: *Astrology for the Beginner*. He recognized it as the volume Boniface had knocked off Pauline's shelf the night he arrived, the one he and Jill had tussled over. Holding the cat securely with one hand, he picked up the book with the other, curious. It fell open to a bookmark, in the middle of the chapter on Virgo.

So, Jill was studying up on him? It gave him a ridiculous rush of pleasure to realize she was interested enough to bother, and then a twinge of uneasiness. What evil things was she learning about him from this book?

He started to put it back down and dismiss it as nonsense. But then he decided, what could it hurt to just take a quick look? He tucked the book under his arm and left before Jill could ask any questions.

Chapter Five

Dinner on the patio was an uncomfortable affair. No one seemed to be enjoying Jill's chicken dish. Stephen ate hurriedly with hardly a word to spare, as if he were eager to get the ordeal over with. Jill, mortified over the impassioned speech she'd made earlier, couldn't meet his eye even if he'd tried to make eye contact, which he hadn't.

"John Phipps called again," Pauline said, at least attempting conversation as she picked at her food. "He said to tell you that the last problem he called you about has been fixed, but now he has another problem."

"Mmm," was Stephen's scintillating reply.

Exactly fifteen minutes after they'd sat down, Stephen laid down his knife and fork, mumbled his thanks and bolted from the table.

"Thank goodness," Pauline murmured as soon as he was gone.

Jill's heart went out to her aunt even as it hardened against Stephen. Ever since he'd come, the older woman hadn't quite been herself. Her perpetual smile had vanished, and she'd taken to spending long periods in her room. "He's making your life miserable, isn't he, with all this budget nonsense," Jill said.

Pauline looked up, obviously surprised. "What? Oh, no, Jilly, not at all. I don't mind the tight finances. I've been poor before, and the prospect doesn't bother me in the least."

"But he's making you sell the beach cottage, isn't he?"

Pauline sighed. "He's just doing what needs to be done, that's all."

"Then why are you mad at him?"

"You've misunderstood. I'm not mad at him. I'm just glad he's gone for the moment. The tension at this table was thick enough to stir with a stick. Tension between the two of you," she clarified. "Oh, Jilly, I've done something terrible by bringing the two of you together. I should have known better. I should have remembered Stevie was a Virgo."

"Auntie, don't be ridiculous!" Jill scolded. "Nothing is going to happen between Stevie—Stephen and me." Although something already had.

Pauline shook her head. "You're wrong. I can feel the sparks between you. There's a heaviness in the air whenever the two of you are in the same room—like how the air feels right before a storm. Something awful is going to happen, I just know it!"

A CHANGED MAN

"I won't let anything awful happen," Jill said as she stood and began to stack dishes with a practical air. "Stephen and I don't get along, that's all. We never have and never will. There is some tension between us—I'm a little angry at him about the beach cottage. But I'll get over it."

"You argued with him?"

"Well, you have to admit he is insufferable at times. Just a while ago he was trying to take over my spice business. You should have heard him—critical as ever, determined to fix something that's not broken."

Pauline finally smiled. "You sound just like you did the time he tried to tell you how to build that model sailboat."

"Oooh, I'd forgotten about that," she said with a renewed surge of irritation. "He hasn't changed a bit, has he?"

"I don't know, Jill." Pauline pursed her lips thoughtfully. "You might at least listen to his suggestions. He's awfully good at what he does."

Jill absolutely refused to admit that Pauline might be right. It was just so hard to face the fact that maybe she did need help, that Spice Up Your Life was starting to get unmanageable. "He's a pest," she said petulantly.

"Jill, honey, do you remember what happened to that model sailboat, the one you wouldn't let him help you with?"

She had to think for a moment. "It sank."

Stephen sat cross-legged on his bed, utterly absorbed. He'd seldom read anything so fascinating, and though it was well past midnight, he couldn't put the astrology book down.

"She can be quite tractable," the book said of the Sagittarian woman, "but don't issue orders to her. She's open to change, particularly if the change is her idea, but she's too independent to allow herself to be bossed around."

Too independent was right, he mused with a grimace. If she were any more so, she could declare herself a separate country.

All right, so maybe he'd been a little heavy-handed with his suggestions regarding her business. Rather than him *telling* her what to do, she needed to discover his ideas on her own, and believe them to be hers.

That gave him a splendid idea. He'd brought along his portable computer from Madison, but so far he hadn't seen a real need to use it. Tomorrow he would find a need.

Stephen reached to turn out his bedside lamp as he closed the astrology book. But some wicked little demon made him open it back up to the section on compatibility. He had to look—he just had to know how he and Jill measured up, astrologically speaking.

"This is not a match made in Heaven," read the first sentence of the chapter on the Sagittarius-Virgo pairing.

Stephen rolled his eyes. He already knew that.

"Virgo's earthy practicality has a tendency to smother Sag's fiery need for adventure," the text continued. "Her footloose, often irresponsible nature can drive the conservative Virgo to distraction..."

Involuntarily, Stephen's eyes scanned down the page to the part about sex.

"On the physical plane, the cool, reserved Virgo would seem a poor match for the playful, frolicsome Jupiter girl. But this doesn't always hold true. If both parties can keep an open mind, the relationship can combine the best of both worlds. Sag's burning, impulsive and sometimes superficial approach to love is tempered—not smothered—by Virgo's cool, deep and tranquil spirit."

Hmm. Stephen wasn't so sure he could describe himself as cool, deep or tranquil when just one touch from Jill made him burn like a Roman candle. But maybe that was simply the result of her fire reaching out to him, stirring up embers that normally burned at a sedate, predictable pace.

He slammed the book closed once more, and this time he forced himself to put it aside for good. Tomorrow he would return it to Jill's apartment and forget about it.

But though he dismissed the subject of astrology from his mind, the image that drifted into his consciousness as he fell asleep was that of a raging forest fire that met a cool, deep lake, creating a delicious, warm steam.

Jill couldn't sleep. It had struck her, just as she was drifting off, that Thanksgiving was little more than a week away, and she still had dozens of nutmeg orders promised in plenty of time for the holiday. That realization had jolted her drowsy mind to wakefulness, and she ended up tossing and turning all night.

By morning she knew what she had to do. She either had to send out a distress signal and get some help, or she would disappoint scores of new customers.

She rose early, a good hour before the time she normally stirred, and called the only temporary employment service in the area. But it failed to dig up even one measly minimum-wage worker on such short notice. With the Christmas shopping season in full swing, demand for temporary help was high. So Jill was left with a most distasteful last resort: she had to swallow her pride and crawl to Stephen.

Pauline obviously wasn't up and about yet, Jill noted as she entered her aunt's kitchen a few minutes later. Hot tea was usually the older woman's first business of the day, and the kettle was cold. But someone was awake. As if she had super-sensitized antennae tuned to Stephen's frequency, Jill knew of his presence in the dining room before she saw him.

She didn't seek him out right away. Instead she filled the kettle and set it on the stove to heat, then pulled three mugs from the cabinet and set a tea bag in each. When she'd procrastinated as long as she dared, she turned and briskly entered the dining room, steeling herself against Stephen's certain censure when she confessed her dilemma.

The sight that greeted her pulled her to a stop. Stephen, looking neat and well groomed as ever in a crisp button-down shirt, worked intently at a computer keyboard. But the computer was like nothing she'd ever seen.

She'd always thought of the machines as cold, impersonal, impossible to relate to. But the screen on this one was beautiful—shimmering in iridescent red, brilliant green, sunshine yellow and cool, soothing blue.

The colors made the columns of numbers seem inviting rather than forbidding.

"What are you doing?" she asked, full of curiosity.

He jumped. "Lord, don't scare me like that. Where'd you come from?"

"Oh, I've been puttering around in the kitchen," she said, evading for the moment the real reason she was here. "What is all that stuff on the screen?"

"I'm just tracking Pauline's expenses over the past twelve months. Thankfully she did keep receipts, religiously it seems."

"Jigs got her in the habit, for tax purposes," Jill said as she pulled out the chair next to Stephen and sat down, dismissing the harsh words she'd hurled at him the night before. Apparently Stephen had forgotten them or was overlooking them. He was certainly more cordial this morning.

"From her spending habits I'm going to determine what her real income needs are," he explained, "so I can decide how to manage her remaining assets. I just enter the receipts, and the computer averages the expenses and comes up with a budget."

"Really? It can't be that easy." She scooted her chair closer, so she could better see the computer. But as he worked, she found her attention divided between the pretty manipulations on the screen and the sight of his fingers working the keyboard. How would it feel to have those nimble fingers working on her?

"Sure it's that easy. Watch. Want to know how much she spent on groceries, per month, over the past year?" He pushed a couple of buttons and the dollar amount appeared at the bottom of the screen, highlighted in red.

"Wow, I didn't know Auntie ate that much." The comment was a lame one, Jill thought, but Stephen's provocative, autumnlike scent was distracting her.

"She has some very expensive tastes, despite what you said about her living simply. She'll have to cut down on the caviar and the filet mignon. Chicken is better for her, anyway. Now you don't think it's unreasonable or unkind of me to recommend that she be a bit more conservative at the grocery store, do you?"

"Mmm, I suppose not," Jill said, resisting a very powerful urge to touch him. "What else can you do with this thing?"

It was almost as if he'd been waiting for the question. He glanced her way, full of anticipation. Then he took a deep breath. "Oh, I don't think you'd be interested. It's dull for someone who doesn't like computers."

"But this is kind of a cute machine," she protested, "not like other computers I've seen. Come on, Stephen, show me what else it can do."

She could have sworn his reluctance was feigned. "Well, take your spice business, for example. Now, I know you're quite satisfied with your, er, rubber-band system, so you probably wouldn't find this at all useful, but you could set up a program—a very simple one, actually—that would allow you to enter each order as it came in, add a few simple codes, and with a push of a button you can call up whatever list you want."

As he spoke, he performed a few simple maneuvers at the keyboard, and up came a box with a list of choices.

"We could even color code them," he continued. "Red rubber band, orders to be filled. Green rubber band, orders to be paid. When a payment comes in, you just push another button, and that member is automatically transferred to the blue rubber band list."

Rainbows of color appeared on the screen.

"The computer will alphabetize, too, and let you know when you're filling a new member's order so you're sure to include a spice rack. It will alert you when an account is overdue. Add an inexpensive dot matrix printer, and it spits out mailing labels."

He made it sound so simple, Jill thought to herself. "What else can it do with money?" she asked, thinking of the one aspect of her business that really frightened her—accounting.

"Lots of things. Call up accounts paid, and you know how much you've taken in that month. Accounts receivable, and you can see what's owed to you. Factor in expenses, and up comes your profit—in green, thank you. It'll make taxes a snap."

She suspected then that he might be snowing her. Nothing could possibly make taxes a snap. Still, something urged her to ask, "How much does one of these little wonders cost?"

"Oh, you could probably get a decent setup for... fifteen hundred."

"Phew! I could buy a lot of rubber bands with that."

Stephen shrugged. "Then stick with what you like, what works for you."

"But I could buy a computer on a payment plan, couldn't I?"

He flashed a sly smile. "You could even lease a system, see how you like it."

"Could I? Who would I call? How long would it take? Could you show me how to make it do all that stuff? Before you go back to Madison, that is." As always, the thought of his imminent departure laid a heaviness in her chest.

"Mmm, I suppose," he answered indifferently. "I'm almost done with the worst of Pauline's finances, but I'll have to stick around for a few more days to tie up some loose ends, so...sure, I'll help out if you really want me to."

"Oh, I do, I..." Had she just agreed to a computer? Why did she suddenly feel she'd been neatly trapped? But as long as Stephen was in this benevolent mood, she'd better do what she came here to do. "Stephen, you know what you said about my spice business getting out of control and strangling me?"

He nodded slowly.

"Well...you were right. I'm not sure where I screwed up, but I've got a couple hundred orders to fill and get to UPS before five o'clock today or I'm going to have some irate customers. I just hate to ask this, but I was wondering if you might be available to lend a hand—if you can spare time away from helping Pauline."

"Of course I'll help you, Jill. I can put off this other work till tomorrow. You just tell me what needs to be done, and I'll do it."

His response was so immediate, so enthusiastic, so seemingly sincere, that it shocked her into silence for a moment. None of the things she'd feared had come to pass. There was no "I told you so," no superior smirk, no strings tied to the offer of help.

Then she remembered something she'd read about Virgos. Theirs was the sign of unselfish service. One of their main purposes in life was to help others, just for the sake of being useful.

She could assign no other motive for Stephen's behavior. What could he possibly hope to get in return? It was a sure bet he wasn't trying to get on her good side for the purposes of physical or emotional intimacy. He'd ruled that out—although she hadn't, not just yet.

"Thank you, Stephen." She would have kissed him on the cheek, or anywhere else he would have allowed, but she had to remember that Virgo men didn't respond well to female aggression. *Patience, patience,* she chanted silently as she settled for running a lingering hand down his arm.

Even that might have been too much, she admitted as she retreated. She hadn't imagined that expression of alarm that flickered briefly in his gray eyes.

The kettle was boiling cheerfully when Jill returned to the kitchen. She made tea and toast for herself and Stephen. A short time later Pauline appeared in her pink-flowered bathrobe, obviously surprised at the scene of cozy domesticity that pervaded her kitchen—and not altogether pleased about it, either, judging from the slight frown she couldn't quite disguise. Still, they all sat at the kitchen table to a much more pleasant meal than last night's.

"You see, there was nothing to worry about," Jill said to her aunt after she'd sent Stephen to change into clothes he wouldn't mind messing up. "Stephen and I are getting along better now. He's going to help me out with a little problem I'm having, and then he's going to teach me how to use a computer."

"Then are you taking his advice?" Pauline asked.

"The computer was my idea," she said, though she knew she was stretching the truth a bit. "After I saw what it could do, acquiring one seemed a natural step for my business."

"Well, that doesn't sound too dangerous," Pauline admitted, just before licking a dollop of raspberry jam off her index finger. "Just so there's nothing else going on."

"Like what?"

"Like...you know, romantic stuff."

"Stephen and me? Oh, no, you must have mistaken him for someone who likes me. Anyway, we're cousins," Jill added for good measure. She figured there was no sense in worrying Pauline about something that probably wasn't going to come to pass, anyway.

"You're cousins-by-marriage, so that has nothing to do with anything. And don't be smart with your elders. I told you I saw sparks, and I'm not senile. There's potential there, whether you admit it or not."

"Yes, ma'am," Jill answered meekly, hoping to forestall further discussion about the subject of her and Stephen. Lying, or even shading the true facts a bit, didn't come easily to her. If Pauline persisted, Jill would eventually blurt out the truth—that she was more than a little attracted to Stephen and that she hoped, probably in vain, that he might respond again to her, as he had at the beach cottage.

"Potential for what?"

Jill and Pauline both stared at Stephen, surprised to find that he'd rejoined them. His immaculate red and white rugby shirt and an obviously new pair of jeans were hardly clothes he should want to get messy, but perhaps that was as casual as he was capable of getting.

"Didn't anyone ever tell you it's impolite to eavesdrop?" Pauline said, neatly avoiding the need for a falsehood.

"It was just girl talk," Jill improvised as her gaze roamed appreciatively over the dark blue denim that hugged his lower torso. He didn't seem the type to wear jeans very often. She wondered if he would use this pair enough that the material would turn soft and faded with many washings, so that it formed itself more familiarly over his anatomy.

Jill shook her head suddenly, wondering what had prompted the barrage of inappropriate thoughts.

"Come on," she said, gesturing toward the door, "let's get started. Four o'clock and the UPS man will be here before we know it."

"Don't worry about lunch," Pauline offered. "I'll throw something together later and call you when it's ready."

As soon as they were in Jill's apartment, Stephen turned to her and asked, "Does Pauline ever help you with the spice business?"

Jill shook her head. "Auntie wasn't wild about this idea when I talked her into financing the venture," she explained. "She made me promise one thing—that she wouldn't have to bail me out if I got into trouble. I can't ask her to help."

"So for one investment of, what, five hundred dollars?"

"Three hundred," Jill corrected him.

"She owns one-quarter of your business, with no further risk?"

"That's right."

"Hmm. She's a pretty savvy businesswoman after all," he said, more to himself than Jill. "So, let's get this show on the road. What do you want me to do?"

Knowing his penchant for neatness, she assigned him the cleanest task. "Take the names and addresses on these slips of paper and write them on mailing labels while I start filling the spice jars."

"By hand? You write mailing labels out by hand?"

She shrugged. "I don't have a typewriter, and I don't know how to type, anyway."

He made no reply to that, but she could almost feel his disapproval as he picked up a pen and got to work.

Jill followed suit, scooping the fine, brown powder from a huge bulk bag and coaxing it through the small mouth of a crystal spice jar via a funnel. She then put a stopper in the jar, cleaned away the excess nutmeg and added a calligraphy label. Next she took a box, filled it halfway with the torn newspaper she used for packing material, carefully arranged the spice rack, jar and recipe booklet inside, filled up the empty spaces with more newspaper, then closed the box and sealed it shut with strapping tape.

When she was finished with a box she set it on the end of the dining room table to await a mailing label, then repeated the whole process.

All the while she worked, she surreptitiously kept an eye on Stephen. He had the most beautiful, precise printing she'd ever seen, so she couldn't fault him on the final appearance of the labels. Hers were sometimes barely legible. But in the time it took him to complete one label, she could have done three or four!

They would never finish at this rate, but she knew better than to ask him to hurry up and write faster. He was quick to find fault in others, and sometimes even in himself, but he hated for other people to point out his shortcomings.

"Why don't we switch jobs for a while," she tactfully suggested. "You must be getting writer's cramp by now."

"Okay," he agreed readily—almost too readily. "I've been watching what you do here, and I think I have it down."

Things went smoothly for a while after that. Jill couldn't help but grin at the method Stephen used. He always spooned just enough into the funnel to exactly fill the jar—no more, no less—so that none of the nutmeg spilled. But his precision was costly in terms of time. Again it took him nearly twice as long to process an order as it took Jill.

She bit her tongue to keep from criticizing. He was bailing her out of a jam, after all. She had no business looking a gift horse in the mouth.

The phone rang, not for the first time that morning. She'd been letting the answering machine handle all calls, as most were incoming orders for Spice Up Your Life. But when she heard Detective Herschel identify himself she hurried to the phone, picked up the receiver and shut off the machine. "Yes, I'm here. It's me. Um, Jill Ballantine."

"Yes, Jill, glad I caught you," Herschel said in his slow, pedantic voice. "I just wanted to let you know that I've done some checking on your D. Z. Ryzinski. It appears Pauline isn't her only pigeon. Ryzinski's had complaints lodged against her from all over Southern California."

"And did you catch her?" Jill asked excitedly.

"Um, no. She doesn't have any previous record, so there's not much information on file—no photo or fingerprints or other aliases. She's probably long gone by now, in another state or even out of the country. We'll keep looking, but I don't hold out much hope. I'm sorry, Jill."

Not half as sorry as Pauline, she wanted to say. "Thanks, anyway," she mumbled before hanging up.

She relayed the information to Stephen, who took the news in stride. "That's what I figured," he said. "Hey, I'm about to run out of packing material."

"I have lots more newspapers on the sun porch," she said, fighting back her frustration. "I'll get them." Everyone had such a pessimistic attitude about catching Madame Zoey, she thought as she picked her way through the living room toward the French doors. Surely *something* more could be done. Maybe they could go on one of those television mystery-solving shows, and make a national appeal. Sometimes crimes were solved and criminals apprehended minutes after one of those shows aired.

"You know," Stephen began when she returned with a stack of papers, "tearing up newspapers is time consuming, not to mention messy. Have you thought about buying those little foam squiggles? They're not very expensive."

"No way," she said in a horrified voice. "It's an environmental nightmare. I'd much rather recycle my neighbors' papers."

"Well, then, how about this. Find a company that uses a paper shredder, and ask them to give you the shreds. At least you wouldn't have to tear it up, and it would be cleaner."

"I'll look into it," she said noncommittally, though perhaps she would take his advice. It wasn't a bad idea. But she didn't want to discuss business just now. Her mind was still on Madame Zoey and how to catch her.

"And I've been thinking about the way you process these orders," he continued. "You waste time and effort by continually picking up and putting down various tools. You'd do better by concentrating on one task. Fill fifty jars at one time. Then put in fifty stoppers. Paste on fifty labels. Pack fifty boxes."

"Yes, I get the idea," she said dryly.

"But don't you see? That way you pick up the funnel only once. You pick up the packing tape only once."

"I understand," she said, this time grinding out her answer. "And we'd save a lot more time if you'd stop flapping your jaws and concentrate on filling those jars."

Silence. Horrible, dead silence prevailed, punctuated only by the grating sound of ripping newspapers and the occasional clink of crystal.

Jill could have slapped herself silly. What had she been thinking, to say something so rude to a man who was unselfishly giving up his whole day just to help her? She hadn't been thinking at all. As usual she'd just blurted out what was on her mind without a thought as to the consequences.

"Stephen?"

"What?" He shot the word out like a bullet, never lifting his eyes from his task.

"I'm sorry. I'm really, really sorry. That was a stupid, nasty, thoughtless thing to say when I know you're just trying to help." She felt a strange tightness at the back of her throat and realized she was about to cry. Over an apology.

She swallowed several times, until she was sure the tears were safely at bay. "Your suggestions are good.

Honestly. What else can I do to make this operation more efficient?"

He looked at her then. Amazingly, the corner of his mouth slowly curved upward in an amused half smile. "That Sagittarian bluntness of yours does get you into trouble sometimes, doesn't it? It's not your fault. You're a victim of the stars."

She narrowed her eyes suspiciously. "How do you suddenly know so much about astrology?"

"I borrowed your book. Okay, I stole your book. I was going to return it this morning, but I forgot. Pretty interesting reading."

"You don't believe in that stuff, do you?" she asked, recalling the part she'd read on how incompatible Virgos and Sagittarians are.

He laughed. "Me? Believe in astrology? No way. But you have to admit, it is amusing. You are the consummate Sagittarian woman—warm and sunny, free-spirited and blunt as a hammer."

"And you're a classic Virgo male," she countered, still digesting his combined compliment-insult. She was planning to say something less than flattering about him and his uptight Virgo tendencies when she remembered she was supposed to be apologizing. She looked down at the newspaper in her lap. "You're right. I am too blunt."

"Forget it," he said magnanimously. "I'll save my suggestions for a more appropriate time, if you're really interested."

"I am interested," she assured him. "In fact, I—Stephen!" She'd been about to tear into a new page of newspaper when an ad had caught her attention.

"Look at this," she said as she popped out of her chair and spread the page out on the table, for Stephen to see. "There's going to be a huge psychic fair in Los Angeles on November twenty-first. That's this Saturday!"

"So?"

"It's the biggest event of its kind in the West," she explained excitedly, paraphrasing the ad. "The psychic event of the year. I'll bet you anything Madame Zoey will be there. How could she resist the temptation?"

"Madame Zoey is probably in another country by now," Stephen argued calmly. "That's what Herschel said."

"Oh, Herschel's an old wet blanket. Why would Zoey move away from California when all she has to do is change her name, alter her appearance slightly and set up shop in a new town?"

"Hmm," Stephen said. "What if she does show up at this psychic fair. How would the police find her if she's using a different name? There's no picture of her available—"

"That's easy. I'm going to L.A., and I'm going to catch her myself!"

Chapter Six

"Oh, no you're not," was Stephen's immediate reaction to Jill's announcement. He could just imagine her traipsing up to Los Angeles, grabbing the phony psychic by the throat and demanding the return of Pauline's quarter million dollars, or else.

Jill fixed her face into a mutinous expression. "Of course I am. How else will we catch that horrid woman?"

"We'll leave it to the police to catch her. Jill, she might be dangerous."

"Dangerous? She's a little old lady!"

"Even little old ladies can get mean when their retirement funds are threatened." He lowered his voice and added, "I don't want to see you get hurt."

His expression of concern seemed to take the starch out of Jill. "All right, then we'll call Herschel. But I don't see what good that will do. Even if Madame

Zoey is at the fair, Herschel won't recognize her. He'll need someone to identify her."

Stephen hated to admit it, but Jill had a point. D. Z. Ryzinski would be smart enough to operate under a different name. And there could be dozens of elderly ladies present at the psychic fair, all matching Jill's and Pauline's rather hazy description.

Jill was already dialing the phone. Stephen sidled up beside her and leaned close to the receiver at her ear, so that he could hear Herschel. But her proximity proved too distracting, what with her wild hair tickling his face and her scent, discernible even over the nutmeg, tickling his imagination. He retreated to a safe distance, settling for a one-sided conversation.

"But of *course* she'll be there," Jill said, twisting the phone cord around her finger. "I just know she wouldn't leave California. No other location would offer her such an assortment of wealthy, um, open-minded sorts to take money from... But this is a *big* psychic fair. Don't you think psychics are like any other professionals—unable to resist these major career-building events?"

There was a long pause, during which Jill twisted and retwisted the phone cord until it was a mass of knots.

"Well, what if I went there and tried to find... but I'd be very careful. I wouldn't talk to her or anything, I'd just look for her. Then if I saw her there I could call you..." Another long pause. "Yes, I see. Thank you, Detective Herschel."

She hung up the phone with more enthusiasm than was necessary, Stephen thought, then put her fists on her hips and glared at him. "Herschel doesn't intend to do anything," she declared hotly.

"Nothing?" Stephen asked.

"Well, he said he'd get in touch with LAPD and have them 'check into it,' but he was just patronizing me. He doesn't even believe Madame Zoey will be at the fair."

"Maybe she won't," Stephen said sensibly.

"But maybe she will. This might be one of our best chances of catching her, and I refuse to ignore it."

"What did Herschel say when you offered to go to L.A. yourself?"

Jill hesitated, as if she wasn't quite sure how much to admit. "He didn't recommend it. He said I ought to leave the investigation to the police. But he didn't forbid it, either. I mean, he can't stop me from simply attending the fair as an ordinary person interested in psychic phenomena."

"Jill..." Stephen warned, thinking that if Herschel didn't stop her, he would himself. The thought of her putting herself in danger sent a forbidding chill up his spine.

"What's the worst that can happen?"

"I have no idea. That's why you aren't—" He stopped, forcing himself to temper his words as he recalled her aversion to direct orders. "That's why you shouldn't go. Please, Jill. Let the police do their job."

"But they won't do their job," she muttered. Then she sighed in apparent resignation. "Do you really think it would be dangerous?"

"Yes," he answered without hesitation. Probably nothing would happen, but there was a small risk, and he wasn't a risk-taker—especially not where safety was concerned. Especially where Jill's safety was concerned. The thought of her confronting a felon made him sick to his stomach. His ulcer might even start acting up, as it did when anything really worried him.

She looked at her watch. "It's time for lunch. Let's go see what Pauline's cooked up for us."

He was surprised she let the subject drop. She didn't mention it to Pauline as they all lunched on chicken salad sandwiches and noodle soup, nor did she say anything about it during the remainder of the afternoon as they processed the last of the spice orders.

He was almost convinced that she'd forgotten all about the psychic fair.

After dinner he heard her jeep start up, then race down the driveway. Jill hadn't said anything about going out, and he was consumed with curiosity about her destination. Pride prevented him from asking Pauline if she knew what her niece was up to.

Did she have a date? he wondered. The possibility bothered him more than he wanted to admit. If she was with a guy, why didn't he come and pick her up? Why hadn't she told anyone where she was going?

Not that a man in her life would really bother him, but he did harbor some protective feelings toward her. With that footloose, devil-may-care attitude of hers, she could easily get involved with the wrong sort. After all, she'd fallen into his arms without much provocation, and a relationship between them would be nothing short of disastrous. She would turn his life topsy-turvy, that was for sure.

He didn't take an easy breath until she returned about an hour later, carrying a large brown sack.

"What's so interesting out that window?"

He jumped at the sound of his aunt's voice. "Jill," he responded as he watched her go into her apartment. "I just wish she'd told me she was going out. I had some letters to mail," he improvised.

"Oh, you know Jill," Pauline said with a careless wave of her hand. "She gets the urge to jump up and go somewhere, and she doesn't give anyone or anything another thought."

"I didn't mean to imply she was inconsiderate," Stephen said, surprised at how quickly he jumped to Jill's defense. "Impulsive, maybe."

Pauline nodded in agreement, which caused Stephen to wonder what her game was. She never, but never, criticized her favorite niece. "She's such a free spirit, it's no wonder she hasn't married. She hasn't even had a steady beau since she's lived here."

Was Pauline hinting at Jill's availability or trying to warn Stephen off? Or was she merely fishing?

"I'm sure she'll find someone, someday," he offered blandly. But it would have to be someone secure enough to accept her independence, he added silently. Someone who was self-confident enough to let her pursue her own interests ... without feeling jealous or neglected, Stephen mused guiltily. Certainly he didn't fit that bill. If Jill were his, he would want to keep her constantly under the protective shelter of his wing, and she would hate that.

"You're not ... interested in her, are you?" Pauline asked.

"Me? You must be joking. She's not my type. Most of the time we're at each other's throats. We've always gotten on one another's nerves." And how many other denials could he come up with?

Pauline appeared decidedly relieved. "I can't see you with someone like Jill," she agreed. "You probably lean toward a more stable, homier type. A nice Cancer woman, that's what you need. Or maybe a Taurus. Have you ever been involved with a Taurus?"

"I, um, don't know. I don't generally require an astrological reference from the women I date." But he was positive he would not be attracted to any woman who took after a bull.

"Well, you should. I'm going to bed now," she concluded cheerily. "Good night."

Stephen sank onto the pink settee. Now just what was that all about? He was still pondering that question when the doorbell rang a few minutes later. It was after eight o'clock. Who would be calling? he wondered as he rose to answer the door.

A frail old woman stood on the front porch, leaning heavily on her cane. Her iron-gray hair was long and scraggly, hanging limply to her shoulders, and the most outlandish hat he'd ever seen sat perched on her head. Her psychedelic-print dress didn't disguise her droopy bosom and a dumpy figure. Worn pink leather gloves, baggy fishnet hose and what looked like orthopedic go-go boots completed the picture.

She squinted at Stephen through thick, cat's eye glasses. "This the Smith residence?" she rasped in a scratchy voice, then craned her neck forward, as those hard of hearing sometimes did.

Stephen looked behind the woman toward the driveway. There was no taxi waiting for her, no unfamiliar cars at all. How had she gotten here? Surely she hadn't walked. She teetered unsteadily just standing on the porch. "No, there's no one named Smith here," he said kindly. "What address were you looking for?"

All at once the woman straightened, and a decidedly youthful laugh bubbled up from inside her.

When reality hit, he could hardly believe what his own eyes told him. "Jill? Jill, it *is* you."

"Yes, it's me," she said as she breezed past him into Pauline's living room. "You didn't have a clue, did you."

"Your own mother wouldn't recognize you in that getup," he said as he closed the door, still amazed at Jill's transformation. She had even put something on her face to obscure her own smooth, youthful skin. "But you're about three weeks late for Halloween."

She flopped down in the cabbage-rose chair. "Not Halloween, silly. I'm planning to wear this to the psychic fair. Madame Zoey will never recognize me. You said yourself my own mother wouldn't know who I was."

Damn! He'd thought she'd given up on this crazy idea. He paced the floor uneasily, trying to come up with a logical objection, but he couldn't latch on to one. "What did you do to your hair?" he asked abruptly. He would have thought it impossible to hide that bright cinnamon color.

"It's a wig," she replied. "I found most of this stuff at a junk shop on Front Street. Come on, admit it, Stephen. This is a good plan. If nothing else, I'll get a charge out of the psychic fair. I've always wanted to check out one of those things."

"It's a crazy plan," he insisted. "But you're going to do it no matter what I say, aren't you?"

She nodded. "I just have to try."

"Then I'm going with you. Someone has to keep you out of trouble."

She laughed at first, but when she saw he was sincere, she sobered. "You mean it? You want to go with me to the psychic fair? Somehow I just can't see you... fitting in. You look too conservative. You'll stick out like... like Clark Kent at a Madonna concert."

"And you'll blend right in, I suppose," he said, nodding toward her outlandish costume.

"I have a feeling eccentricity is the norm at one of these shindigs." She gave him an appraising look. "I suppose we could jazz you up a little. Maybe a tie-dyed T-shirt—"

"No way," he said firmly. "I'll go as I am, so save your breath. People will just have to think I'm your conservative... son."

She giggled at that. "All right. I suppose I could do worse in the way of a partner."

Partner? He viewed himself more as a chaperon or bodyguard, an unwilling party to this harebrained scheme. But if she wanted to think of him as a partner, an accomplice in the search for truth and justice, he'd let her, if for nothing else than to keep the peace.

There had been far too little peace between them, and he rather liked it on those rare occasions when they were in accord.

The psychic fair wasn't nearly as odd as Stephen had feared. In fact, the Convention Center on Pico Boulevard in central Los Angeles appeared as if it was in the middle of just another trade show. Booth after booth lined the cavernous hall, each neatly numbered, most bearing tasteful signs. Plain fluorescent lights illuminated the hall. Innocuous music—New-Age stuff, Stephen suspected—floated gently among the psychic fair's patrons.

Even the attendees didn't appear out of the ordinary for the most part. They just looked like a cross-section of Californians—young, old, some flamboyant, some conservative and a few downright weird.

The woman walking next to him was one of the weirdest, and she garnered a few curious looks. But most people hardly glanced twice at her.

"You see, everyone just dismisses me as another eccentric," she said under her breath. Then, in her louder, old-woman voice, she added, "Let's go get our palms read, Stevie."

Stephen grimaced at her deliberate use of his despised childhood nickname. "Yes, *Mother*," he replied through gritted teeth. He hadn't actually expected to participate in this hocus-pocus stuff, but Jill had insisted that if they didn't, they would look suspicious.

At four or five dollars per consultation, this "investigation" of theirs was going to get expensive.

Stephen listened with half an ear while a young, studious-looking man read Jill's palm. The man spouted the usual vague generalizations about Jill's supposed past and her character, based on what he thought was her age and a few false cues Jill herself gave him. He was far off the mark.

"See what a lot of nonsense this is?" Stephen whispered after they left the palmist.

"I never claimed to believe in it," Jill whispered back. "Then again, not all psychics are as bad as he was. Madame Zoey was much more convincing than that."

They wandered through crystal displays, demonstrations of past-life regressions, mind reading, psychokinesis and psychic healing. There were booths offering instantaneous computerized horoscopes and on-the-spot dream analysis. One could purchase self-help books and tapes on improving psychic abilities or learning astral projection.

Stephen found the whole subculture frankly fascinating. That people would actually believe this stuff... Although wasn't he only one step away from this himself? Hadn't he been reading an astrology book with at least some small degree of belief? Hadn't he convinced himself that understanding Jill's astrological sign would help him to understand her and deal with her more effectively?

Not only that, but it was working. He ought to be careful whom he criticized.

It seemed they'd been pacing the huge exhibit hall for hours—and in fact they had, Stephen noted when he checked his watch. But Jill insisted they cover every inch of the place so she could check out each face. "We didn't go to all this trouble just so I could carelessly overlook Madame Zoey," she pointed out as they rested at a snack bar, munching on organic salads.

Reluctantly he agreed as they resumed their search. But he was growing bored with the whole thing and so dropped back a couple of paces behind Jill, to give himself something to look at. Even while affecting her fake old-woman hobble, her rounded hips swayed seductively. And the fishnet support hose couldn't conceal the shapely curves of her legs. How had he ever been fooled, even for a second, into believing she was an old woman? She positively oozed youthful vitality.

They passed a booth where a man offered to take special photographs of his customers, revealing "the spiritual presences surrounding you."

"I can't believe people are still falling for that old trick," Stephen couldn't help observing aloud. "Photographers have been taking those so-called 'spiritual' photos since Victorian times. They've been proved a hoax."

"Oh, will you stop being so practical?" Jill complained as they entered a large section of the exhibition hall devoted to Tarot card readers. "Granted, Madame Zoey took gross advantage of Aunt Pauline, but most of these exhibitors are sincere, and the people attending the fair are just having fun. You should get a reading done, just for the entertainment value. You don't have to take it seriously."

"I'll pass, thanks."

"Come on, humor me. I'll even pay for it—" She stopped abruptly as she looked past Stephen, and her eyes grew wide behind the cat's eye glasses. She pulled the spectacles off her face and let them dangle on a chain against the droopy padding of her false bustline. "Stephen!" she hissed. "I think I see her."

Stephen started to glance over his shoulder, but Jill grabbed his arm.

"Don't look!" she warned with what he thought was an excess of caution. "Wait till she's looking the other way... okay, it's safe."

Stephen turned and peered inside the large, striped tent which housed perhaps a dozen card readers, each presiding over his or her own table. "Which one?"

"The third one down on the left, with the black hair. She has a sign over her table that says Wynndora."

"Are you sure it's her?" he asked.

Jill hesitated. "No. I'll need to get a closer look."

Immediately Stephen's caution reasserted itself. "How close?"

"If I could just get inside the tent..." She paused to think. "I know. We'll ask for one of the other readers. Then we can stroll by this Wynndora person's table and I'll be able to tell for sure."

"I don't know, Jill," Stephen objected. "You promised me and Herschel you wouldn't get close to her."

"I said I wouldn't talk to her," Jill said as she dragged Stephen by the arm toward the man who guarded the entrance to the tent. "There's a difference. Excuse me, sir," she said in her old lady voice, "my son would like a Tarot reading with—" she quickly read the sign on the table not too far from Wynndora's "—with Lily of the Valley."

The man, dressed something like a sultan, smiled back at them. "Certainly. Lily happens to be free right now. That'll be seven dollars."

Stephen's eyes clearly expressed his displeasure as Jill extracted the money from her green patent-leather handbag. She smiled sweetly up at him.

Lily was the only psychic Valley Girl Jill had ever seen. She appeared to be barely out of her teens, with long, blond hair, a beach-bunny tan and purple leggings. She squealed a lot as she did a card layout for Stephen. Jill sat beside him, with one eye trained on Wynndora, two tables down.

The older woman *looked* a lot like Madame Zoey. But the hair color was different, as were the glasses. The clothes were less flamboyant, the makeup less pronounced. Jill just couldn't be sure.

"Like, your aura's really powerful, you know?" Lily said to Stephen. "I can feel it, like, almost vibrating it's so potent, you know?"

Stephen nodded uneasily.

Jill waited until Wynndora finished with her latest customer. Then, without consulting Stephen, she stood and casually hobbled to the older woman's table.

Wynndora fixed her with a sudden, penetrating stare, and at that moment Jill knew Wynndora and Madame Zoey were one and the same. Then the older woman smiled with false benevolence. "Can I show you something of your future?" she invited.

"Oh, well, uh," Jill wavered. "I don't have any more cash on me."

Zoey's smile dimmed only slightly. "That's all right," she said, shuffling the worn deck of oversized cards. "I'll just take a quick peak. Then, if you think it's worth something, you can send me a few dollars." She pointed to a stack of her pastel pink calling cards, which sat on the table.

Jill's heart stampeded inside her chest even as disgust rose in her throat. Old ladies appeared to be Madame Zoey-Wynndora's specialty, and she was very persuasive—frighteningly so.

"Is there a problem?" Stephen had come up behind her, and his voice reeked of censure.

Jill clamped her hands around his arm. "Mad—uh, Wynndora wants to give me a free reading." Damn, she'd almost said *Madame Zoey!* This undercover stuff was proving harder than she'd imagined. She was panicking during a crucial moment.

"I don't think—" Stephen started to say.

But the old woman was faster. "It won't take long. Here, shuffle the cards," she said, holding out the dog-eared deck toward Jill.

Before Jill knew what was happening she had the deck in her hands. To object now might seem odd, she decided, and she didn't want to draw any closer scrutiny from their quarry. "All right," she said, making sure her voice was extra-scratchy and deep in her throat. "Just a quick peek, now." She settled in the chair across the table from Zoey, clumsily shuffled the cards with her gloved hands and gave the deck back to her.

Stephen sat next to Jill, his body as stiff and tense as the tent poles that suspended the striped canvas above them. He was plenty upset with her, that was for sure. She'd have some explaining to do when they got out of here.

"Let's see what we have here," Zoey said thoughtfully as she peered at the cross-shaped display of cards laid out on the table. "You've had some family troubles, perhaps concerning money, yes?"

Jill cleared her throat and nodded.

"I thought so," Zoey said triumphantly. "Are you by any chance a Pisces?"

"I'm a Sagittarius," Jill couldn't help saying. She wanted to knock Zoey and her phony fortune teller skills down a peg.

Stephen gave her a warning look.

"Sagittarius?" Zoey asked as she removed her glasses and studied Jill. "That doesn't seem...are you sure?"

"Of course I'm sure," Jill said, tipping her head down and averting her eyes.

Zoey shrugged as she again looked at the cards. "I just get this feeling of secrecy and hidden meanings from the cards, and that usually goes with Pisces. Sagittarians are generally so open and honest, they can't hide anything when they lay out the cards...." Her voice trailed off as she looked up once again, and her expression gave Jill a wicked shiver up her spine.

"Could we get on with this?" Stephen interrupted impatiently. "I have an appointment to get to."

Zoey's eyes burned with an unnerving intensity as she stared at Jill, almost trancelike. "You're Pauline's Sagittarius niece." She turned quickly to Stephen. "And you're the Virgo! I tried to warn Pauline. There's blood and death—oh, heaven help the two of you!"

Before Jill or Stephen could react with more than open-mouthed stares, the unearthly light seemed to fade from Zoey's gaze, leaving her once again just a plain old woman. Then her perceptive eyes narrowed as she realized the implications facing her. Fast as a shooting star she tipped the table into their laps, whirled around and fled through an opening in the tent. The colorful Tarot cards flew in every direction.

"What was that all about?" asked Lily, who had come over to investigate the disturbance. She helped Jill and Stephen set the table upright. "I swear, that woman has a nasty habit of stealing my clients, you know?"

Jill and Stephen didn't wait to hear the rest of Lily's complaints. They both took off at a dead run after Madame Zoey.

"There she is!" Stephen shouted, pointing toward the woman's back as she made her hasty way through the crowd. "Boy, she moves fast for an old lady." He ran after her and Jill followed, hampered by her high-heeled boots but still managing to keep up.

They pursued Zoey to an exit, which led to a concrete stairwell. Pausing at the top of the stairs for just a moment, they could hear the clunk of her shoes one or two flights below them. They followed relentlessly. When she reached the lowest level she was forced to exit into the parking garage. Her progress was easy to mark, and they were gaining on her.

Jill had no idea what they would do when they caught up with her. Wrestle her to the ground? They would probably face assault charges if they did that, never mind Zoey's own criminal activities.

The woman was obviously heading for her car. Maybe they could catch the license plate and have Herschel trace her that way.

Jill was still running strong by the time they reached the garage. She could see Zoey's portly form, bouncing ahead of them down a long row of cars. She felt a surge of triumph, which was quickly displaced by blind panic as her spike heel caught in a crack in the pavement and she went flying. Her ankle twisted painfully as she hit the concrete with a thud.

"Jill?"

She looked up to see Stephen skidding to a stop.

"Never mind me," she said breathlessly. "Go after Madame Zoey."

"Are you okay?"

"Yes! Stephen, you're losing her!"

He turned toward Zoey as she disappeared around a corner. Then he looked back at Jill, still in her unladylike sprawl. His indecision was plain.

"Just go!" she urged desperately, though suddenly she didn't really want him to leave her there. The sharp pain in her ankle brought tears to her eyes.

Stephen shook his head as he closed the distance between them and knelt beside her on the concrete, touching her face in a gesture of unexpected tenderness. "Oh, Jill, what have you done to yourself?"

She tried to smile through her tears of mixed pain and frustration. "Turned my ankle, that's all," she said. "I'm sure it's nothing. Dammit, Stephen, she's getting away." They heard a car engine start, but from their vantage point couldn't see where it was or where it went.

"Forget Zoey," Stephen said. "I grabbed one of her business cards. Maybe Herschel can trace her with that. Let's take care of you. Which ankle is hurt?"

"The right one," she said as he eased her into a more comfortable sitting position. She unzipped her boot and together they worked it gently off her foot. The ankle was swelling fast.

"We better get some ice on that," he said as he scooped her into his arms.

"Stephen, I can walk."

"With your ankle swelling up like a cantaloupe? I don't think so. In fact, I think we better get it X-rayed."

"No, really, that's not necessary. Besides, we need to call Herschel and let him know what we found out so he can get right on it."

"We'll call him from the hospital."

"But I don't have any medical insurance," she protested again, though she sensed that she did so in vain. Stephen was determined to take care of her, and there didn't seem to be anything she could do about it. He couldn't help it, she told herself. She remembered reading that Virgos were drawn to the weak and helpless.

"We'll take care of the fee one way or another," he said in a soothing voice. "Don't worry about it."

Finally she gave up arguing, put her arms around his neck and laid her head on his shoulder. His solid body against hers felt warm and reassuring, and she decided it wasn't so bad, letting him take care of her. Though these weren't the exact circumstances she would have chosen, at least she was in Stephen's arms again.

It felt good.

Chapter Seven

Jill left the Good Samaritan Hospital emergency room on crutches, two hundred dollars lighter in the purse. Her ankle, swollen to the size of a softball, throbbed relentlessly, as did the scrapes on her knees and elbows.

She figured she looked worse than she felt, even after disposing of the wig, hat, glasses, gloves and most of the false padding. At least she hadn't broken any bones. She could thank the Lord for small favors.

"So, was Herschel impressed that we found Madame Zoey?" she asked Stephen as he helped her into the passenger seat of his rental car. He had called the detective to tell him the latest while Jill was getting X-rays.

"*Impressed* isn't quite the word I would have picked," Stephen replied. He waited to elaborate, until he was seated behind the wheel and had started the engine. "He did perk up a bit when I told him we'd located D. Z. Ryzinski, but he wasn't exactly thrilled by how we handled the situation. We spooked her good, so she'll be gone by the time he can trace the phone number from her business card. She'll also be more careful next time about where she surfaces. She might actually leave the state or even the country."

"So we probably made the situation worse instead of better," Jill said glumly.

"Maybe not. Just the same, Herschel made it pretty clear that he wants us to cease and desist with our investigative efforts."

Guilt ate at Jill's conscience. She hadn't handled herself well at all. "I didn't mean to let Zoey know we were on to her," she said. She didn't care what Herschel thought of her, but she wanted to make Stephen understand. "All I did was walk by her table. She's the one who started up the conversation. And I tried to discourage her from looking at my cards, but she's so darn persuasive... I'm really sorry," she concluded miserably. "I guess I should have believed you when you warned me that something bad might happen."

Stephen reached over and gave her arm a squeeze, allowing his hand to linger for a few delicious moments. "Don't worry about it, Jilly. What's done is done."

She couldn't have been more surprised—not only at his easy forgiveness, but at his use of her nickname. It sounded almost like an endearment, the way he said Jilly, and for the first time she liked the familiar tag.

"I was under the impression that you were furious with me for getting too close to Zoey," she said carefully. "The way you looked at me when you found me talking to her..." Jill shivered at the memory. There had been no compassion, no understanding in his clear gray eyes.

Now he actually smiled at her. "I was pretty irritated at first," he admitted. "But then I realized you were right about Zoey. She's extremely charismatic, not to mention manipulative. I don't doubt that she reeled you in like a fish on a hook." He paused, scowling at the traffic ahead of them. "She even had me going for a minute."

"You mean what she saw in the cards?" Jill asked, finally broaching the subject they'd both been avoiding. "That was weird, all that stuff about secrecy and deception."

"It was even more weird that she recognized you," Stephen said. "She must have a helluva memory and incredible observation skills."

"That might explain how she saw through my disguise, but Stephen, how in the world did she know you were a Virgo? She's never met you—probably never even *heard* of you. I doubt she learned anything about you from Pauline. Auntie even told me she hadn't remembered you were a Virgo until you showed up."

Stephen shrugged, though Jill could tell the question bothered him more than he let on. "Zoey had a one-out-of-twelve chance of guessing right," he said.

"Not very good odds. And she wasn't guessing—she *knew*. It was like she saw the truth in those cards. Then there's that thing about 'blood and death'—"

"Let's not even ponder the possibilities," Stephen said firmly, his hands tightening on the steering wheel.

"She's a skilled con artist, and she was trying to unnerve us, that's all, so she could get a head start."

"Well, she certainly succeeded," Jill said. "She gave me a first-class case of the willies." She paused to look out the car window, realizing with a start that they were on Sunset Boulevard, headed into Hollywood. "Where are you going? This isn't the way back to Del Rosa. We need to get on the Santa Ana Freeway."

He sighed. "You aren't looking forward to that long drive home, are you?"

"Not really. Why?"

"I thought we might find a hotel and stay in the city tonight. It's late, we're both exhausted, and you really ought to rest and elevate that ankle."

She was intrigued by the idea. Sharing a hotel room with Stephen...although surely he meant *two* rooms. If they shared a room, resting would be the last thing on her mind. Mmm, he might even be able to take her mind off the pain of her injury.

"Sounds good to me," she said, forcing as much casual disinterest into her voice as was humanly possible. "I'm sure if we head toward the airport, we can find someplace reasonable."

Stephen turned to look at her with a mischievous twinkle in his eye. "Reasonable? Nothing about this entire day has been reasonable. Why should we start now? Name the swankiest hotel you can think of—we'll stay there."

"Oh sure, we'll just pull up under the canopy at the Beverly Palms, toss the car keys to the valet, waltz in and get a room—with me looking like a horror-movie reject."

"No, of course not." He paused dramatically. "We'll get a suite."

To Jill's amazement, that's exactly what they did.

The Beverly Palms Hotel was unutterably extravagant, with its elegant cream and rose decor and silk-upholstered furniture. Stephen paced the pale rose carpet, soft enough to sleep on, as he waited for Jill to finish with the bubble bath she'd insisted on when she saw the glamorous bathroom, a confection of gilt and porcelain.

His decision to stay the night here had apparently surprised the stuffing out of Jill. It wasn't like him to part with his money on a whim, she'd pointed out. Even when they were kids, he'd always managed to make his allowance last the whole week, while she spent hers the first day. But hell, he'd put aside some money for a vacation, he rationalized, and he wasn't spending much of it staying at Pauline's house and eating chicken salad sandwiches.

Besides, he wasn't quite ready to let go of Jill. Once he got her home, she would again be preoccupied by her mail-order business, and he would have to finish straightening out Pauline's finances. All too soon his job would be completed and he would be on his way back to Madison. He wanted this one night with Jill— one peaceful night when nothing and no one was making any demands on either of them.

Not that he intended to do anything except talk to her and maybe pamper her a little. He just wanted to get his fill of her company, that was all. Anything more would be unforgivably foolish. They simply weren't compatible—even the damned astrology book said so.

Even Madame Zoey said so.

That didn't stop him from wanting her to the point of near obsession. It seemed like the harder he fought his desire for her, the more potent it became. When he'd picked her up and held her close in that parking garage, the only thing that had prevented him from kissing her right then and there was the fact that she was hurting. The need to get her to a hospital had overshadowed his own, more personal need.

"Stephen? Hey, Stephen, are you out there?"

Even muffled through the bathroom door, her voice tickled his senses. "I'm here," he answered. "Something wrong?"

"Can you bring me one of those pain pills the doctor gave me? I think they're on the coffee table."

"Sure. Is your ankle worse?" he asked worriedly. She hadn't kept ice on it the way she was supposed to.

"It's throbbing a little. But what really hurts is my head. Peering through those prescription glasses all day didn't do me a bit of good, and that itchy wig didn't help, either."

Stephen found the medicine and returned to the bathroom door, then hesitated as he reached for the knob. "You want me to come in . . . there?"

She laughed at his reluctance. "Of course, silly. How else can you give me the pills? Anyway, I'm quite decently covered from my neck to my toes."

He slowly opened the door, not completely trusting her. It would be like Jill to deliberately shock him, just to see his reaction. But when he peered cautiously inside the bathroom, he found that her body was indeed modestly concealed by mounds of bubbles in the huge, sunken tub.

But bubbles or not, the sight of her reclining in the tub was arousing in itself. Her glorious auburn hair was spread out behind her on the edge of the tub, forming a wild tangle of fire against the cool, pale rose porcelain. He was so entranced by the sight that it took him a few moments to realize she was holding out her hand, waiting patiently for him to give her the pain medication.

Quickly he placed one of the tablets in her palm, then gave her a glass of water.

"Mmm, thanks," she said after she'd gulped down the medicine. "Stay and talk to me for a while, at least until the pain pill kicks in."

Part of him wanted to stay. The fact that she'd deliberately requested his company pleased him all out of proportion. But common sense told him to get out of that intimately steamy, floral-scented room as fast as possible. She was naked under those bubbles, for heaven's sake, and the frothy layer of suds that covered her would soon start to thin out. Would he have the willpower then to make a timely exit?

"I need to call Pauline and tell her where we are," he said, knowing full well the excuse sounded manufactured. It was. He had already warned his aunt that they might not be back until tomorrow. He'd known even before their unfortunate encounter with Madame Zoey that he wanted to stay the night in L.A. "I thought I'd order from room service," he added as he paused at the door. "What sounds good?"

"Mmm, anything. Steak, hamburger, pasta—I don't care, just so long as it's not an organic salad. Could you hand me my hairbrush before you go? It's by the sink."

Illogically his heart sank. She could have at least tried to talk him into staying, instead of so blithely accepting his first refusal. She didn't even sound disappointed.

Stop thinking like an idiot, he berated himself as he reached for the brush and started to hand it to her. But at the last minute some devilish urge took control of his better judgment.

He'd been itching to get his hands on Jill's unruly cinnamon locks. When would he ever have a better opportunity? He sat down by the edge of the tub and started brushing her hair himself. There was nothing he loved more than bringing order to chaos.

She tensed briefly when he first touched her hair. He began slowly, giving her every opportunity to object, but she said nothing, and after a few minutes she relaxed and gave herself up to his ministrations.

Her hair was incredibly soft. He worked patiently at each tangle, reveling in the feel of the silky strands as they brushed against his hands and wound themselves around his fingers. The snarls were definitely a challenge, but he'd never enjoyed a task more.

She sighed as he worked, and her obvious pleasure only added to his own enjoyment. When he was nearly done he slowed way down, drawing out the last of the job, savoring each moment. Or perhaps he was merely extending the anticipation, because he knew that when her hair was free of tangles, he was going to put down the brush and kiss her. His better judgment was not only severely hampered, it had gone right out the window.

Jill settled herself more deeply in the cooling water and suppressed a moan of pleasure. She had always enjoyed having her hair styled at a salon, but Stephen's gentle hands were a hundred times better than those of an impersonal hairdresser. Each time his fingers brushed the back of her neck, she shivered all the way down to her toes. The tiny muscles of her scalp virtually quivered at his touch.

She had no idea what had prompted him to do such an uncharacteristically impulsive thing, but she wasn't about to question it. She'd begun to think she would never move this reserved Virgo man, that she would never again see that streak of sensuality she'd glimpsed at the beach house. But his actions now were definitely sensual. In fact, he was thoroughly seducing her. She wondered if he knew the effect he had on her. Were his actions truly prompted by impulse, or was there some premeditation involved?

She imagined him pressing his face into her hair, his warm breath rustling the smoothly untangled strands. She imagined him leaning down to kiss her ear, and running the tip of his tongue along the inner curve. Then suddenly she didn't have to imagine anymore. His face was before hers, his eyes smoky with desire, and she knew a sharp thrill of anticipation like nothing she'd ever felt before. Her stomach muscles tightened and her toes curled as he cupped the back of her neck in his palm and leaned closer....

At the first contact of his lips with hers, she thought someone had turned on the whirlpool jets. But it was her body, not the water, that vibrated with electricity as his mouth moved hungrily against hers. Her skin became ultrasensitive to the feel of silky suds against it, to the hard, smooth porcelain at her back. Even the sound of tiny bubbles popping seemed magnified.

As many times as she'd relived in her memory the kiss they'd shared at the beach house, nothing had prepared her for the white-hot passions brought on by the real-life feel of his nearness, his breath mingling with hers, his hands strong and sure against her flushed skin. His pure animal vitality filled her with a unique brand of energy and awareness so keen it almost hurt. Her senses were pushed to the limit as emotions too strange and wonderful to name pushed at the inside of her heart, threatening to burst it wide open.

He slid one hand down the side of her face, her neck, her shoulder, then under the water to boldly caress one water-slicked breast. The increased intimacy seemed as natural as breathing, and Jill knew, even through the hazy cloud of desire surrounding her, where they were headed. The prospect of sharing her body with him sent a new thrill coursing through her.

She wanted to feel more of him. She wrapped her arms around his neck, pulling him closer. If she'd realized how precariously he was balanced above her, she might have tempered her enthusiasm. As it was, the only warning she had came too late. Stephen parted his lips from hers and gasped, wide-eyed with surprise, just before he plunged fully clothed into the water with her.

Jill's roiling emotions coalesced into one huge and totally inappropriate reaction: she laughed. She tried not to, but the sight of Stephen's rare lack of composure struck her as so hilarious she couldn't suppress the giggles that rippled up from deep inside her. Even when she slapped her hand over her mouth, the laughter bubbled forth right between her fingers.

Stephen raised up on his knees, straddling her between his legs, as rivulets of bubbles rolled down his previously neat, blue button-down shirt.

Jill's eyes traveled lower, to his sopping wet khaki trousers. The material clung to him with uncompromising thoroughness, revealing the exact degree of his desire—or lack thereof. Obviously the tepid water had doused his passion.

She snapped her eyes back up to his face, and her laughter faded as quickly as it had materialized. He was not a happy camper.

He never said a word as he pulled himself out of the water and grabbed one of the huge monogrammed bath towels to dry himself. He fairly vibrated with anger, and his reaction seemed exaggerated to Jill. Pulling him into the tub had been an accident, after all.

"Stephen, don't go away mad," she said, attempting to cajole him out of his suddenly foul humor. "I thought you looked good in bubbles."

"I don't find this amusing," he finally grated out. "But I suppose I got exactly what I deserved for..." He couldn't quite bring himself to describe what he'd done.

"What is the big deal?" she couldn't help asking. "So you got wet. Is that such a tragedy? If you ask me, it would do you some good to loosen up a little. I know how you Virgos hate messing up your clothes, but you're acting like a stuffy old stick-in-the-mud."

"I didn't ask you. And it might do you some good to curb your impulses once in a while. Do you ever think before you do something crazy? Do you ever censor your thoughts before they come right out of your mouth?"

"Curb *my* impulses?" she asked, incredulous. "Just who, in your opinion, started that kiss?" If he even insinuated that she'd "offered herself" to him, she'd leap right out of this tub and slug him.

"I admit that my poor judgment is to blame. But I can assure you it won't happen again," he said stiffly.

"That's what you said at the beach cottage."

"Dammit, I'm not trying to initiate a discussion here," he said as he blotted the water out of his slacks with short, choppy movements. "Just drop it. I'm going to forget the last ten minutes ever happened, and I suggest you do the same." With that he swept out of the bathroom and slammed the door behind him, although his dramatic exit was diminished somewhat by the squish-squish of water in his leather shoes.

She jumped out of the tub and limped after him, trailing bubbles behind her and leaving wet footprints across the plush rose carpet. She jerked the door open. "It's a discussion whether you like it or not, and I'm not going to let you walk out in the middle of it," she announced to his back. "It wasn't all my fault that you got wet, and it's entirely unfair of you to say such nasty things to me just because *you* regret your own impulsiveness."

He whirled around, his finger raised, ready to argue the point, when something sucked the wind out of his sails. His eyebrows flew up in surprise and he turned away from her again before speaking in a tight, almost choked voice. "For God's sake, Jill, would you put some clothes on?"

By George, she was naked, she realized as she looked down at herself. Oddly enough she wasn't embarrassed. She felt no compulsion to grab a towel and cover herself. Still, she couldn't hope to launch an effective argument in such a state. Without another word she retreated to the bathroom. Obviously she needed to think a few things through before she charged at Stephen with half-formed arguments and said something she'd regret.

She vigorously shampooed her hair, attempting in vain to remove the vestiges of Stephen's touch. By the time she finished, the urge to argue with him passed, and another emotion, a heavy, foreboding one, settled onto her chest like a lead weight.

This wasn't going to work.

Stephen's falling into the bathtub, and their respective reactions, perfectly illustrated the irreconcilable differences in their outlooks on life. Stephen saw his impromptu swim as a terrible blunder, nothing less than total ruination of his carefully orchestrated seduction. She, on the other hand, couldn't help but see the accident as funny. He would never understand her playful approach to physical intimacy, and she would likely find it impossible to adjust to his more serious, almost somber attitude.

If they couldn't even put aside the basic differences in their natures when they were in each other's arms, what hope was there that they could successfully mesh other, even more glaringly contradictory aspects of their lives?

She wished now that she'd listened to the warning that damned astrology book had issued about Virgo-Sagittarius compatibility, instead of allowing herself to explore and to hope. Her hopes had just been dashed to bits.

Wrapped in a plush rose-colored robe she'd found on the back of the door, Jill cautiously exited the bathroom, hopping on her good ankle. Stephen would no doubt still be pacing and fuming. She intended to calmly offer an apology for her "impulsive" behavior and her rash words. She would assure him that she, too, planned to forget the entire incident. Then, if he was any sort of a decent human being, he would apologize for overreacting and for insulting her, and they could get on with life.

But when she hobbled into the suite's living area, Stephen wasn't pacing *or* fuming. He was seated on the couch, wearing a robe identical to hers and calmly reading the newspaper.

He looked up. "Does your ankle feel better?" he asked. It was as if nothing out of the ordinary had passed between them.

"Yes, it's fine," she answered distractedly. She settled onto a chair across from him and worked at re-wrapping her ankle with an elastic bandage as she formulated her next words to him, although her plan of action didn't seem to fit the situation anymore. "Stephen, I'm terribly sorry about your clothes."

He smiled blandly, his eyes still trained on the newspaper. "That's fine, Jill. There was no real harm done. I sent the clothes out to be cleaned, and they'll be back first thing in the morning."

That was it? What happened to all that anger, all the sparks that had been arcing between them like an electrical storm? Not that she wanted him angry with her. But anything would have been preferable to this horrid aloofness. His studied indifference stung almost more than his hurtful words.

"I hope you like prime rib," he said. "That's what I ordered from room service."

"Wonderful," she replied feebly. "Prime rib is perfect."

What else could she say? Apparently he really had purged the last few minutes from his memory. Certainly no apology was forthcoming.

They shared yet another tense meal. This was getting to be a habit, Jill thought as she tried to swallow the prime rib. Stephen assured her the food was delicious, but it was lost on her. Her senses were dulled. All she could think about was the chance she and Stephen would never have. Physically, only a few feet of the glass coffee table separated them. Emotionally they were miles apart.

She wanted to dismiss her disappointment as easily as Stephen had. But a niggling, insistent voice inside her kept reminding her how marvelous it would be to surrender herself to Stephen, to let him surround her with his potent masculinity, to submerge herself in his... his powerful aura, to use Lily of the Valley's terminology.

So, they were destined never to be lovers, never to more fully taste the unique passion between them. It seemed such a damned waste. Yet who was she to argue with the all-knowing stars?

"Don't you like the chocolate mousse?" Stephen asked as he watched Jill pick at her dessert. Normally she had a healthy appetite, yet tonight she'd hardly touched her food. He wondered if her ankle was bothering her more than she let on. Even that prospect was preferable to what he guessed was a more realistic explanation: she was upset, extremely so, and it was all his fault.

"It's okay," she replied, laying down her fork. "Guess I'm not all that hungry. In fact, I just want to go to bed. I'm so tired."

Tired of dealing with him, he supposed. He could be a tedious person when he wanted to be. But how else would he keep her at a safe distance? That was the way it had to be—that, or he would keep on making the same stupid mistake, succumbing to her wholesome, sunny sexuality.

Taking Jill to his bed would be the worst thing he could do to her. She might believe in living for the moment, but the moment would eventually end. He couldn't stay here much longer—John Phipps wasn't handling the practice well on his own, and Stephen's secretary was ready to commit hara-kiri with his overflowing message spindle.

Neither could Jill come with him to Madison. Even if she wanted to leave California, she couldn't abandon Aunt Pauline, not now when the older woman was so vulnerable. There just was no possible way anything could work out.

"You can take the bedroom," he said. "I'll sleep out here. The couch folds into a bed."

She nodded curtly, bid him a terse good-night and hobbled away.

Stephen spent an uncomfortable night on the too-small sofa bed. By morning he could hardly wait to get out of the luxurious suite, which had become his own plush prison. He rousted Jill out of bed with a loud knock on her door, and by eight-thirty they were in his rental car and headed south on the Santa Ana Freeway.

Jill hardly spoke on the way home. Her continued silence worried him, even though he knew he was the cause of it. He wanted to comfort her, to somehow convince her that they were better off as adversaries than lovers. But he didn't dare even bring up the sensitive subject. His own feelings were still too close to the surface, and too unpredictable, for him to trust himself.

When they finally turned down Pauline's long driveway, they found her weeding the garden out in front of the pink stucco house. When she saw them she jumped up with a spryness that belied her age and went straight for the passenger side of the car.

"Jilly Bean!" she cried as soon as Jill opened her door. "How is your ankle, poor dear? Stephen told me last night that you'd taken a spill."

"Hello, Auntie. It's not too bad," Jill answered, giving her aunt a dutiful hug. "I suppose Stephen told you the rest of the news, too?"

"You mean about almost catching Madame Zoey?" Pauline shuddered. "If I'd known you would come face to face with that horrid woman, I never would have approved of you going to the city in the first place."

"What's done is done," Stephen said, the same words he'd used to comfort Jill when she was feeling guilty over her part in Madame Zoey's escape. Now the phrase seemed to take on added significance, as if he was trying to tell her there was no going back, that the rift between them was irrevocable.

She glanced at him with sad, reproachful eyes before returning her attention to Pauline. "You shouldn't be out here working in this heat," she scolded, setting aright the older woman's pink straw hat, which their hug had knocked askew. "Let's go inside and get something cold to drink."

"Wait, before we go inside," Pauline said, "I'm afraid I have some rather disturbing news of my own." She hesitated, then plunged on. "Boniface somehow got into your apartment, Jill. He, uh, knocked one of the cages down and ate a pair of the finches before I caught him."

Jill's hand flew to her mouth in a horrified reaction.

"I'm so sorry—" Pauline said, but her apology was lost on Jill, who was already tearing off at an awkward gait toward her apartment, to view the damage herself.

Stephen started to follow her, but at his aunt's warning look he stopped.

"Let her grieve in peace for a few minutes," Pauline advised. "And don't feel too badly about it. She has so many finches that they aren't exactly pets, they're more like inventory. She'll cry a little, because it's sad when a small, helpless thing dies, but she'll be fine."

Stephen sagged against the car. "Blood and death," he murmured.

Pauline's eyebrows flew up. "I beg your pardon?"

"Madame Zoey. She said something about blood and death coming between Jill and me."

Pauline shivered again. "Zoey might be a harpy, but occasionally she does hit the nail on the head. Come on, Stevie, let's go inside. I could use a cold drink. And I have another piece of news for you—good news this time. I think you'll be pleased."

Chapter Eight

"Someone is interested in buying my house," Pauline announced when she and Stephen were seated at the kitchen table with tall glasses of iced tea in front of them.

"That *is* good news," Stephen agreed, "especially since we only put it on the market a few days ago. Have you received an actual offer yet?"

Pauline was shaking her head. "I'm not talking about the beach cottage. I mean this house. That real estate agent called while you were gone yesterday, and we had a long chat. Such a nice young man! Anyway, since he was already familiar with *this* house, I asked him what he thought it was worth, and he said he knows of a buyer who would plunk down a million dollars for it in the blink of an eye. A million dollars! Can you imagine that? That's probably ten times more than Jigs paid to have it built—"

"Whoa!" Stephen held up a hand to halt his aunt's monologue. "Pauline, don't get carried away. You don't have to sell your house, for heaven's sake. I've found several other assets you can liquidate—T-bills, stocks, a life insurance policy on Jigs. Once the beach cottage sells, you'll have a comfortable income. Besides, where would you live if you sold this place?"

"I'm working on that," Pauline said. "And why shouldn't I sell this house? I've lived here for more than twenty years, and that's longer than any Sagittarian likes to stay in one place."

"What about Jill?" Stephen asked, sure that Pauline hadn't even thought about displacing her niece. "Where will she go if you sell?"

To his surprise Pauline smiled sagely. "Oh, I think I know where Jill will go," she said, but she didn't elaborate. "Speaking of Jill, why don't you go see how she's doing? Poor dear," she added with a click of her tongue.

He frowned at the reminder of the mishap with Jill's birds. "I think I will," he said as he stood and drained the last of his iced tea. Walking out the kitchen door, he noticed the ripped screen and realized with a surge of guilt that he was to blame for his cat's transgression. He'd known the screen had a hole, and Boniface had demonstrated on several occasions his craving for finch. Stephen should have done something to prevent the accident.

He found Jill on her sun porch, sitting in a deck chair with an empty bird cage in her lap. She looked so dejected, his immediate impulse was to go to her, hold her, comfort her. But he quickly nixxed that urge.

One false move and he'd be right back in the same mess he'd been in last night— with Jill in his arms and no timely dip in the tub to return him to his senses.

Would that be such a bad thing? He tamped down the unwelcome thought as he cautiously approached Jill.

She didn't look up, though he was sure she heard him. He knelt by her chair and grazed his fingers along her arm. She glanced over and back, barely acknowledging his presence as she pulled away from his touch.

"Are you okay?" he asked.

"What do you think?" she replied woodenly.

"I think you look pretty sad."

"I am sad. Two tiny, helpless creatures were slaughtered."

"I know, and I'm sorry. Bloodthirsty beast," he added.

Jill sighed, and a tear slipped from the corner of her eye. "Oh, I don't really blame Boniface. He was just doing what comes naturally to cats, just following his instincts."

"Then I guess I'm to blame for not fixing the torn screen that he escaped through."

She looked at him then, more curious than angry. "You're so meticulous about everything else. Why did you let that slide?"

He shrugged. "Busy with other things, I guess. I'll be happy to reimburse you for—"

"Oh, that just figures," she cut in, suddenly fuming. "I'm sure you think money will solve everything. Just pay Jill for the little dead birds and she can buy new ones, right? Just buy her an expensive prime rib dinner and she'll forget all about—" She didn't finish. She didn't have to.

So that's what this was all about, Stephen mused guiltily. She'd been so quiet last night and this morning, and he'd had a feeling she was holding something back. She was obviously upset over more than just her deceased finches.

He couldn't blame her for being ticked off at him. But she was more than angry, he realized. She was hurt. He'd never seen her looking so vulnerable, and he just couldn't help himself—he had to touch her, even though he knew she wouldn't welcome comfort from him just now. He reached up a hand to smooth her cinnamon hair away from her face.

As he expected, she shied away from his hand, but he wasn't prepared for the look of pure contempt she shot his way. It stunned the breath right out of him.

"Just don't, Stephen," she hissed. "I'm not a yo-yo you can drop and then pull back to you at your whim. Get out of here and leave me alone."

Her sudden attack left him speechless. But she wasn't about to soften her defensive stance. He could tell by the hard set of her jaw, the resolute clench of her fists.

Fine, then, he would leave her to stew in peace—for now.

Jill watched Stephen go with a mixture of sadness and longing, but still satisfied that she'd done the right thing. It had taken every ounce of her willpower not to accept the comfort he offered. But a saner, more analytical part of her knew how harmful his tenderness could be, when he decided to pull it away again.

She had no doubts that he desired her. He might even feel something deeper for her, on an emotional level. But the fact remained that he had rejected her—twice. And last night he had seduced her and *then* rejected her. He'd been cold and hurtful because it suited his purpose at the time. Not only had he berated her for her actions, he had attacked her very nature. She couldn't subject herself to that kind of hurt again.

Stephen had assured her that there would be no more passionate moments between them. This time, she wouldn't trust him to keep his word. She would make very sure that he didn't get close enough for passion to flare.

She wasn't really angry over his cat's indelicate meal-taking. The fact was she was the one who had left a window open. She was as much to blame as anyone for the loss of her birds. But the unfortunate accident would make a handy excuse for keeping Stephen at arm's distance.

If she could maintain a healthy head of steam during the remainder of his stay in Del Rosa, then he would never know, never guess, that she was falling in love with him.

It occurred to Stephen, as he patched Pauline's kitchen-door screen a few minutes later, that he'd made a gross error in judgment last night.

He hadn't been able to help that first surge of anger when he'd fallen in the tub. He'd felt like a fool, and Jill had laughed at him. But later, after he'd thought it through and realized his graceless slip into the water wasn't her fault, he should have apologized for acting like an ass. Then, if the Fates had been kind, he and Jill could have taken up where they'd left off.

Instead he'd made light of their passion, pretending the kiss was insignificant. That had seemed such a sensible, practical course of action at the time. He'd thought to save them both from a foolish mistake. The last thing he'd wanted to do was hurt her with his feigned indifference. But obviously he had.

And for what? Some high-and-mighty notion on his part that he knew what was best for her as well as himself. In his infinite wisdom, he had decided to ignore the strongest biological and emotional pull he'd ever experienced, simply because a match between himself and Jill seemed ... unlikely. Impractical.

Maybe for once he should have followed her lead and to hell with convention. Maybe he should have lived for the moment, then lived with the consequences. If it didn't work out between them, they would survive. He and Jill were both strong people. And if it did ... the possibilities awed him.

But how to win her over, when he'd done everything but drive her away with a stick?

He needed help. It wouldn't hurt to pray, he supposed. A little divine intervention would be welcome. And as long as he was enlisting help from Heaven, he might as well include the stars, too. He still had the astrology book, which he'd never returned to Jill. Maybe some more thorough reading would lend inspiration.

Later that afternoon, after he'd progressed as far as he could with Pauline's budget, he allotted himself some study time. Stretched out comfortably in a deck chair by the pool, with a tumbler of iced tea at his elbow, he opened the astrology book in his lap to the chapter on Sagittarius.

He had only read a few paragraphs when he became aware of a continuous *snip, snip, snip* sound. He looked up to see Jill limping around the side of the house with hedge clippers, trimming Pauline's evergreens with what seemed an excess of energy.

Stephen hoped her strenuous efforts would work off some of that anger. "Sagittarians are slow to provoke," he had just read, "but once pushed past their limit their tempers can explode like a gasoline fire—and anyone who crosses their paths can get singed. But the flames usually burn themselves out quickly, and the sunny archer can hardly remember what the fuss was all about."

Jill's flames weren't burning out quickly enough to suit Stephen's taste, he thought as he chanced to look up. He caught her gaze, and she nearly seared him with eyes that appeared less tranquil and more electric blue than they usually did. The sound from the clippers had changed from *snip, snip, snip* to *whack! whack! whack!*

"Aren't you supposed to be working on Pauline's budget?" she demanded.

He smiled back at her, determined not to let *her* provoke *him*. "I can't do anything until the banks open tomorrow," he answered pleasantly. "But I should be finished in a day or two. I guess you'll be glad to see me go."

"You *and* your carnivorous cat," she snapped.

He tried not to wince. Obviously she needed more time to chill out. He returned his attention to his book, although he couldn't help looking up from time to time just to watch Jill work in her tiny shorts and a bikini top. With every *whack* she made with the clippers, her hips wiggled just—so.

After a few minutes he put the book aside, discouraged. He was covering material he'd already read, and nowhere in this book did it advise him how to deal with a Sagittarian woman in a stubborn temper.

"You look like you could use a refill."

Startled, Stephen looked up to see Pauline with a fresh glass of tea, which she set on the table next to him.

"Oh, thanks," he said with genuine appreciation. "But you don't have to wait on me."

"I was coming out here, anyway," she replied with a shrug. "I also wanted to give you these." She plunked a stack of books onto the table. "I noticed you were reading that beginning astrology book, and I thought you might be interested in some additional materials, something a little more sophisticated. Well, I think I'll go help Jilly with the trimming," she continued quickly, then strolled away before Stephen could object that he was only thumbing through the astrology book to pass the time.

Just the same, he perused the new titles. One slim volume caught his attention: *Astrology for Lovers*. Was it a coincidence that Pauline had placed it on top of the stack? He'd been sure his aunt was dead set against any entanglements between himself and Jill. Had she changed her mind?

He hoped so. Pauline would be a powerful ally in his campaign to win Jill's heart.

It didn't take long to find exactly what he was looking for in the *Lovers* book. "The Sagittarian woman may brag that she has a heart as tough as shoe leather, but don't kid yourself. It's an act. Fact is, that heart of hers bruises as easily as a ripe peach—if she cares about you."

She was definitely bruised. Did that mean she cared about him?

"If you refuse her love once, she might never offer it to you again. But there are ways into her heart, if you are persistent and sincere. Try a grandly romantic gesture, for starters. Although she pretends to shun sentimentality, she is a romantic to the soul. She cries over flowers and mushy greeting cards."

Hmm. Stephen couldn't see himself giving her something as impractical as flowers, but a gift of some kind sounded like a good idea. He could buy her that computer she wanted...

No, that wouldn't be tactful at all, he decided. She would only accuse him of trying to cram his business methods down her throat. Or of trying to buy her forgiveness.

Something less expensive, perhaps, but more romantic. He thought for a moment, then snapped his fingers as inspiration struck. Perfect! He would take care of it first thing in the morning.

Stephen had to drive practically all the way into San Diego to find the store he sought, in a huge shopping mall. He could have asked Pauline for directions to a more convenient location, but he didn't want his aunt spilling the beans and spoiling his surprise for Jill.

Now that he was in the pet store, standing before a massive wall of bird cages, he wasn't sure this was such a brilliant idea. The array of finches was mind boggling, and he knew nothing about how to choose a pair.

"What sort of finches are you trying to replace?" the young saleswoman asked.

"I have no idea," he replied. He hadn't thought to ask, and he hadn't examined any of Jill's birds all that closely, so he didn't really know what they looked like.

"Well, we have zebras, societies, cutthroats, spice finches, waxbills, orange cheeks—all the common varieties," the clerk said as she pointed to various birds.

The tiny creatures fluttered and darted around their cages so quickly, Stephen couldn't tell one kind from another. Their incessant peeping made him nervous, too. They weren't the most personable creatures in the world, he decided.

"Well, let me know when you've decided," the clerk added as she sidled away from him, probably searching for greener territory. The pet store was packed with holiday shoppers, eager to spend money.

Stephen turned his attention to some of the other breeds of birds. One pair in particular caught his attention—two small, brightly plumed, parrotlike birds. They sat close together on their perch, heads touching. Their tranquility contrasted sharply with the frenetic activity of the finches, and he was drawn to it.

"Peach-faced lovebirds," the sign above their cage read. Lovebirds? Did he dare give Jill such a suggestive present? Then again, he was trying to plant suggestions in her head, wasn't he?

He located the clerk, who was showing a Lhasa apso puppy to a couple with two squealing children. "I'd like to buy the lovebirds," he blurted out before he could convince himself to be sensible. Lord knew he'd been much too sensible already where Jill was concerned.

"Lovebirds?" The saleswoman raised her eyebrows.

"Don't ask questions, just wrap them up for me," he said with an embarrassed smile.

He hadn't literally meant to "wrap them up," so he was surprised when the clerk removed the birds from their cage and stuffed them into small cardboard boxes. "Can't you put them in a cage or something?" he asked. He couldn't give the birds to Jill in a box.

"They travel better this way," the clerk explained patiently. "But if you don't already have a cage, we sell all kinds here—also food dishes, toys, mirrors..."

By the time Stephen left the pet shop, he'd talked himself into a small but ornate brass cage, several toys and enough food to last the lovebirds into the next century. He could have put a healthy down payment on a computer for all the money he'd spent, but he refused to think about that. Money wasn't the issue here. His sole objective was to bring a smile to Jill's face, and he hoped this would do it.

On the way out of the mall he passed a card shop. He hesitated by the entrance, then figured *what the hell,* and went in. He'd gone this far, he might as well make a complete fool of himself.

He'd thought the finches posed a confusing choice until he saw this place. Aisle after aisle of greeting cards—big ones, small ones, funny ones, sentimental ones, some adorned with flowers, some with cartoon characters. How was anyone supposed to make a decision?

He was on the verge of walking out in pure frustration when one card in particular caught his eye. As soon as he saw it and read the sentiment inside, he knew it was *the perfect* card. He paid for it quickly, then got out of that mall before some other wild impulse took hold of him.

By the time he arrived back at Pauline's house, keeping his purchase a secret became impossible. The serene little birds started up with the most ear-piercing shrieks Stephen had ever heard.

"What in the world?" Pauline asked as she rushed into the living room, where Stephen was trying to transfer one of the recalcitrant birds from its box into the cage. "My word, I thought someone was being murdered."

"Stubborn beasts," he muttered as he finally managed to stuff the bird through the brass door of its new home.

"It's a lovebird!" Pauline exclaimed, obviously charmed as she bent over the cage. "Oh, how precious. For Jill?"

"I damn sure wouldn't own the things," Stephen answered. Now that he had the technique down, getting the second bird into the cage wasn't as difficult.

As soon as the two were reunited, they proceeded to shriek at each other, causing a deafening din. What had happened to those serene, tranquil creatures he'd seen at the pet shop?

"Oh, they'll settle down in a bit," Pauline assured him. "They're just having a lovers' spat."

"I don't know," Stephen said dubiously. "If Jill doesn't already despise me, she might hate my guts if I give her these obnoxious little monsters."

Pauline laughed delightedly. "Trust me, these birds are just the thing to cheer her up. There's not an animal in the world that won't worm its way into that girl's heart. Why, I even caught her petting Boniface this morning."

The cat in question wandered into the living room just then, and his scarred ears perked up at the sight and sound of live prey.

"Oh, no you don't," Pauline scolded as she scooped him into her arms.

"You can lock him in my room for a few minutes," Stephen said, "until I get these birds safely in Jill's apartment."

"She's not home right now, you know," Pauline informed him as she scratched the surly old cat behind his ears to quiet him. "She decided to spend the morning at the beach. But I'm sure she wouldn't mind if you just set the cage inside the front door. That way she'll have a nice surprise waiting for her when she gets home.

"Oh, I almost forgot—I have a message for you. That nice young man, John Phipps, called. Your business partner, right? He said it was something urgent."

Everything was urgent to John, Stephen mused with a roll of his eyes. "All right. I'll call him back in a minute." But first he had a gift to deliver, and a card to sign.

As he stood in Jill's living room a few moments later, trying to decide what to write on the card was almost as taxing a decision as choosing the card itself. He finally just scribbled a few inane lines—what did he have to lose?

Jill drove toward home later that afternoon, sunburned, exhausted and no closer to the peace she'd sought than when she'd left that morning. Funny, a few hours at the beach cottage had never failed to calm her spirit on previous occasions. But if anything, she was even more agitated than before.

She had to do something about Stephen. The longer she pretended to be angry with him, the worse she felt about her charade.

She couldn't let him go home to Madison without telling him how much she'd come to care for him. Not that her declaration would make any difference. She simply wasn't the type of woman Stephen wanted or needed in his life, and he would no doubt be embarrassed at her revelation. But still, she had to make her feelings known.

His rental car wasn't in the driveway when she arrived home, a distinct disappointment. She wanted to talk to him now, before her courage deserted her. But at least she'd have time to get cleaned up before she confronted him, she reasoned as she entered her apartment.

She knew something was different as soon as she closed the door behind her. An unfamiliar chirping noise drew her into the living room, where she immediately saw a bright brass cage and its colorful occupants, sitting on her coffee table.

She barely had time to recover from the shock of finding a strange pair of lovebirds in her apartment than another surprise jolted her: a pale orange envelope was propped against the cage, addressed to "The Cinnamon Girl".

She supposed that meant her. Stephen had called her that once before, during one of their rare moments of closeness. She opened the envelope with trembling hands.

On the front of the card was a brightly colored drawing of several items on a cutting board—a clove of garlic, a pepper mill, sprigs of parsley and small jars of oregano, basil and rosemary, according to their labels.

When she opened the card, she had to laugh. "You spice up my life," the inscription read. But tears choked her laughter when she read the words Stephen had written himself: "Some people say it with flowers. I say it with lovebirds."

For any man to buy such a frivolous, romantic gift for a woman would be cause for celebration, but Stephen? He was a Virgo through and through, practical to the bone. She knew exactly what it cost him to make such a gesture. Apparently she'd been wrong about him—he did care, no matter how hard he'd tried to pretend otherwise. He cared enough to defy his own basic nature in an effort to please her.

She giggled through her tears as her own feelings bubbled to the surface. This was almost too good to be true! He cared about her, and that was just one step away from loving her. She literally skipped to the bathroom, intent on bathing and grooming herself to unparalleled perfection. Fate was giving her one more chance with Stephen, and this time she would have every advantage she could muster in her corner.

An hour later, wearing crisply pressed cotton slacks and her nicest blouse, her hair tamed into a neat French braid, and trailing the faint scent of Chanel No. 5 instead of her usual nutmeg, she walked across the carport to Pauline's kitchen. Stephen's car still wasn't back, but he was sure to return soon, and she intended to be waiting for him.

"Oh, you're back," Pauline greeted her with less than her customary enthusiasm. The older woman was mixing batter for blueberry muffins, one of Jill's favorites. "I guess I didn't hear your jeep."

"I had the muffler fixed. Where's Stephen?"

"Oh, Stephen— Did you like the lovebirds?"

"They're wonderful," Jill said, smiling broadly at the reminder of Stephen's thoughtful gift. "And don't tell me you didn't have a hand in that. He never would have picked them out himself."

Pauline shook her head in denial. "No, no, I had nothing to do with it. His idea completely."

"Then I can't wait to thank him. Where is he?"

When Pauline looked up, the expression on her face was so tragic, Jill was sure someone had died. "Oh, Jilly Bean, he's gone. He went home to Madison this afternoon."

Chapter Nine

Even as Jill tried to summon rage over this...this betrayal, tears sprang to her eyes. "But he couldn't have left without..."

"I'm afraid he did," Pauline said softly as she put aside her wooden spoon to lay a comforting hand on Jill's arm. "There was some sort of emergency at his office. He had to get back right away. In all fairness to Stephen, he did wait as long as he possibly could for you to come home, so he could see you before he left."

"While I was whiling away the hours at the beach cottage, thinking I had all the time in the world! Oh, Auntie, this is terrible!" Jill wailed as she sank into a kitchen chair.

"It is? But I thought you didn't even like Stephen."

Jill gave her aunt an appraising look. "I think you know better."

Pauline smiled shyly. "Yes, I guess I do. We Sagittarians have a hard time hiding our feelings, although you gave it a pretty good shot."

"Too good," Jill said with a shake of her head. "Stephen thinks I despise him."

"Give him some credit, Jilly. He's not that dumb."

"If he's not that dumb, then why did he leave without a backward glance?"

"He didn't want to. I could tell that. But he didn't have any choice. Fortunately you do, my dear. You could go after him."

Jill's jaw dropped at the sheer audacity of Pauline's suggestion. "You mean follow him to Madison and announce that I'm madly in love with him? He would run screaming into the woods."

"Maybe, maybe not," Pauline said thoughtfully. "You'll never know until you try it."

Jill shook her head in denial. "I couldn't. I couldn't leave my birds, and the spice business—and you. You need me here, especially now."

"The birds and the spices will be here when you get back. I'm suggesting a short trip, for now. But as for me..." Pauline pulled out a chair and sat down, taking Jill's hands in hers. "Jill, honey, you know how much I've loved having you with me these past two years. Why, I don't think I could have gotten through everything without you."

"And I've loved every minute living in Del Rosa. You helped me out, too, you know. You gave me a means of moving away from my parents and gaining some independence without my having to hurt their feelings."

"So, it's been a beneficial arrangement for both of us," Pauline agreed. "But the time has come for you and me to move on." She hesitated, then plunged ahead. "What I'm trying to tell you is that I'm selling this house. I received a firm offer this morning, and I'm going to accept."

Sell the pink house? "You're kidding. Oh, Lord, you're not kidding!" Jill scarcely breathed the question as she tried to assimilate this surprising bit of news. "But where will you live?"

"I'll move back to the beach cottage. You know how much I love it there. Oh, I know it needs work, but so many things about it remind me of Jigs. I can almost feel him there, sometimes."

"Aunt Pauline," Jill said with alarm, "you don't actually believe—"

"No, of course not, dear." Pauline placed a reassuring hand on her niece's arm. "I know Jigs is well and truly gone now. But I think I'll be more comfortable with my memories in that quiet little house, where it all started. Now don't worry. I won't spend all my time moping about, living in the past. I intend to travel."

"Travel?" Jill repeated numbly.

"It's what I've always wanted to do. When I was young I was too poor. And when Jigs and I finally did have some money, we were too tied down. Now, for the first time in my life, I'm truly free and I intend to take advantage of it."

At Jill's doubtful expression, Pauline added, "I know I've made some poor decisions in the past, but I'm stronger now. Near bankruptcy shook me up a little, and made me see things more clearly. I'm strong enough to go it alone for a while—and smart enough not to let anyone take advantage of me again."

"Oh, Auntie, I think you *should* travel, if that's what you want." Jill enveloped Pauline in a warm hug, relieved to see her aunt sounding so sane and sure of herself. "But I guess that means I'll have to move out."

"If the sale goes through, yes," Pauline agreed. "My point is, as long as you're moving, why not move to Madison?"

Jill shook her head. "I don't think that would go over well with Stephen. You know those Virgos. They don't appreciate aggressive pursuit."

Pauline clicked her tongue and shook her head. "Jill, I'm surprised at you. You shouldn't let all this hocus-pocus astrology nonsense influence your behavior. It's fine as an amusement, but don't let it rule your life. Oh, I know, I'm one to talk. But I believed in Madame Zoey with all my heart and soul, and look where it got me—broke!"

"You mean you don't believe in astrology anymore?"

Pauline shrugged. "I'm not sure. But I do know one thing. I wouldn't let it stop me from chasing down the man I loved and bringing him to heel!"

Jill giggled at the mental picture of herself, chasing Stephen down the street, tackling him to the ground and putting a leash on him. But then she sobered. "Even if I didn't know a thing about his Virgo nature, I still wouldn't go after him. I've tried being forward with him, and he really doesn't respond well.

When it comes to a relationship—he wants to set the pace. He'll come around when he's good and ready, when he's prepared to deal with me on that level, and not a moment sooner."

"That's a Virgo, all right," Pauline agreed.

"Anyway, I thought you abhorred the idea of Stephen and me getting together."

"I did, at first," Pauline admitted. "Madame Zoey did predict that a Virgo man would bring you pain and sorrow, after all. But he's already done that, if those tears threatening to spill out of your eyes are any indication. I figure the worst is over. There's nothing more to fear."

"That's one way of looking at it," Jill said glumly.

"If you're not moving to Madison, where *will* you go?" Pauline asked. "I don't like the idea of leaving you in the lurch."

"Oh, don't worry about me. I'll think of something," she responded, dashing away her silly tears with the back of her hand.

Just when Jill thought she couldn't handle any more surprises, she received a dilly of one. The phone was ringing when she returned to her apartment a few minutes later, and she found Detective Herschel on the other end of the line.

"D. Z. Ryzinski, alias Madame Zoey, alias Wynndora, is in custody," he informed her without preamble.

"You're kidding! How did it happen?" Jill asked. "Did the business card help?"

"The phone number on the business card was just an answering service," he explained, "so that wasn't much of a lead. But we were able to trace her through her booth rental at the psychic fair."

He didn't bother to offer Jill even a word of thanks for all she'd gone through to get him that information, she thought with a small surge of resentment. He was probably taking credit himself for conceiving the brilliant idea of checking into the psychic fair.

"What about Pauline's money?" Jill asked.

"There's a fair possibility at least some of it will be recovered," Herschel replied, "but tell her not to go spending it yet. It could be months, even years, before we straighten out this mess. Oh, there's just one more thing... Ms. Ryzinski wants to see you."

Jill gulped. "Me? Whatever for?"

"She said something about 'putting her mind at ease.' You don't have to, of course. But if you do want to see her, she's being held temporarily at the county jail in L.A., until she can post bond."

There was no question in Jill's mind, she realized as she hung up. Although the prospect of facing the spooky Madame Zoey again sent a forbidding chill up her spine, Jill would grant the old woman her request, if for no other reason than to satisfy her own burning curiosity.

It wasn't until two days later, the day before Thanksgiving, that Jill found the time to visit the jail. She'd never been inside a prison before, so all she knew was what she'd seen on television. She was therefore surprised when the authorities allowed her and Zoey to meet very informally, in a small room furnished with a simple table and two chairs. If not for the bored-looking guard standing by the door, Jill would have thought she was simply visiting an elderly acquaintance at a retirement home.

The appearance of D. Z. Ryzinski herself was a bit of a surprise, too. Devoid of makeup, with her graying hair brushed back from her plain face, she could have been anybody's grandmother. She certainly didn't appear to be a master criminal.

Jill had to revise her opinion when she got a look at Zoey's steely eyes, however. The older woman couldn't hide the acute intelligence that lurked behind her temporarily subdued demeanor.

"I suppose you think I'm just a washed-up old con artist, don't you," Zoey began.

"I think you're despicable for preying on an old woman's grief," Jill replied, not pulling any punches. "You *should* be locked up—not just for stealing her money, but for giving her false hope with your fakery. She honestly thought she was communicating with Jigs."

"How do you know she wasn't?" Zoey countered as a look of amusement crossed her features. Then she frowned. "I may very well be a thief. That's for the legal system to decide. But I'm not a fake—not all the time."

Jill raised a skeptical eyebrow at that.

"Oh, I can't claim that everything I do for my clients is genuine. Sometimes the real intuition just doesn't come through, so I have to make something up. But I do have frequent flashes of insight that simply can't be attributed to the five senses. How do you think I knew who you were, under that disguise? And how do you think I recognized that Virgo man you were with? You know I'd never met him."

"I'm sure a logical explanation could be found," Jill said stiffly.

"Believe what you will," Zoey said, folding her hands on top of the table. "I didn't invite you here to convince you of my abilities. I merely want to ask you a question. When I saw you and the man together, I got a definite impression of death surrounding you—blood and death. It's very rare that a message comes to me with that much intensity. So please, put an old woman's mind to rest and tell me—*what happened? Did someone die?*"

Jill almost laughed aloud. Poor Zoey really was concerned. Whether she had any psychic abilities or not, she certainly believed she did. And Jill was almost inclined to agree with her.

"Birds," Jill said. "Stephen's cat ate two of my pet birds while we were in Los Angeles. That's the only blood and death I know about."

"Oh, thank heavens!" Zoey appeared genuinely relieved as she slumped back against her chair. "Yes, that makes sense. It could have been birds. The vision never specifically indicated people." The sudden smile she turned on Jill was almost beatific. "Thank you for coming here and telling me. I really was worried."

"Well, you don't have to worry any more," Jill said stiffly as she rose, eager to terminate this visit. She was half afraid she would again fall victim to the woman's charisma. "The Virgo has gone back to Wisconsin, so he can't possibly cause me any more trouble. I doubt I'll ever see him again."

She turned to leave the room, but Zoey's voice, eerie sounding in the sudden quiet, halted her.

"You're wrong about that," was all she said.

Jill still fought the shivers caused by the old woman's words as she climbed into her jeep. But the prediction, uttered with such certitude, also gave Jill a slender thread of hope.

Zoey had nothing to gain with her parting statement, so she *must* have seen something in her mind's eye, regarding Jill and Stephen. Then again, Jill mused, the old woman might have a vindictive streak. Suppose she'd said what she had just for the pleasure of giving Jill false hope?

Nonetheless, possibilities chased themselves around in her head as she drove home. Maybe she *was* destined to see Stephen again. Suppose she went to Madison, as Pauline had suggested. She could relocate her mail-order business without too much trouble. And the finches—well, they'd probably have to go, she thought with only a mild sadness. The tiny creatures were extremely susceptible to cold; one power outage on a winter day would make them history.

As for Stephen? She could let him know that she was nearby, without pushing. Under no pressure, he might eventually come to realize he loved her.

"Oh, get a grip, girl," she chastised herself. Stephen hadn't even called since he'd gone home. He couldn't be as anxious for a reunion as she was. He'd likely as not forgotten about her already.

Not only had Stephen not forgotten about Jill, he missed her terribly—crazy Jill, with her wild cinnamon hair and her outlandish way of looking at things. The concise, orderly life he'd built for himself now seemed cold and empty, as did his house. Even Boniface was moping about.

"I should have left you behind," he mumbled to the cat. "I think you liked it in California."

Pauline, who had grown rather fond of Boniface, had offered to keep him. But Stephen, who had once pledged to keep the ill-tempered feline only until another home could be arranged for, had found it impossible to part with the cat. Funny how feelings could spring up between the most unlikely creatures.

As if sharing his master's thoughts, Boniface jumped into Stephen's lap in a rare show of affection. His orange eyes glowed reproachfully, as if pleading to go back to that warm, abundantly birdful place.

"I didn't have any choice in the matter, okay?" Stephen said, wondering why he was justifying himself to a cat. He'd hated leaving Del Rosa with things so unsettled between himself and Jill, but his immediate return home had been unavoidable. For once, the problem his partner had called about was an actual catastrophe. One of their firm's larger clients was undergoing a routine IRS audit, and some very peculiar discrepancies were popping up. Since Stephen had personally handled this client's taxes, his input on the matter was essential until he could convincingly demonstrate that his accounting firm had nothing to do with any wrongdoing. So he'd booked passage on the first available flight to Chicago, connecting to Madison.

The worst of it was that once he got things caught up here, he couldn't manufacture much of an excuse to return to California. Pauline's finances were pretty well squared away. He had her bank accounts in order, a reasonable budget established and a modest income to take care of her until the beach house was sold. Mr. Kingston at the bank was fully apprised of her financial situation, and he could answer any questions or handle any problems that cropped up.

But did Stephen need an excuse to call? He reached for the phone, then stopped himself from picking up the receiver, for probably the tenth time that day. The temptation to at least hear Jill's voice was almost overpowering. But he had already gone pretty far out on a limb with his gift. The next move had to be hers.

She might not make a next move, he acknowledged with a wistful sigh. He couldn't blame her if she refused to take any more chances on him, after the mess he'd made of things.

Perhaps it was better this way, he thought glumly, trying to console himself. With some time to herself, maybe Jill's anger would mellow. Then, when they crossed paths again—and they would, he didn't doubt that—they could start fresh.

When the phone rang he jumped, for his hand still rested lightly on the receiver. It was probably John again, wanting further news of the ill-fated audit. That, at least, was going well. Their client was in a heap of trouble, but Stephen's tax work was beyond reproach.

The phone rang a second time before he picked it up. "Hello?"

"And you thought you'd gotten me out of your hair."

"Pauline!" he exclaimed, genuinely pleased. He'd missed his aunt almost as much as Jill. "You're not having any more problems, are you?"

"No, no, I just wanted to bring you up to date. They caught Madame Zoey, and I might even get some of my money back. Someday."

"That's fantastic!"

"And I thought you'd want to know—I've sold the pink house, and I'm planning to move to the beach cottage and live there. Naturally I've taken the cottage off the market."

Stephen wasn't sure how to react to that. She'd gone directly against his recommendation, a fact that should have irritated him, under normal circumstances. But he hadn't been thinking or acting normally for quite some time now. Anyway, the deed was done, and he found himself latching onto the very convenient opportunity she'd unwittingly offered. Or not so unwittingly, he realized.

"If that's what you want, then I'm happy for you," he said, meaning every word. "What will you do with all your furniture? It won't all fit in the beach house."

"Gracious. I hadn't thought of that," Pauline said. "I could have a garage sale, I suppose."

"Now that's quite an undertaking. You can't do it all yourself, of course. You'll need help sorting and packing and pricing, not to mention help with the actual move. I could come first of next week."

"Oh! That was easy. I thought I'd have to twist your arm."

He laughed at that—as if anyone would have to force him to take advantage of a bona fide excuse to see Jill again. "How's Jill doing?" he couldn't help asking, although he attempted to make the question sound casual.

"Jill is... well, Jill is Jill. You'll just have to see for yourself. Have a happy Thanksgiving."

Pauline's words piqued his curiosity so thoroughly, it was all Stephen could do to wait until next week to return to Del Rosa. He wondered about Jill all through the tediously formal Thanksgiving dinner at his parents' home and all the next day, through two rousing football games and several rounds of leftovers at John Phipps's house.

Stephen was so nervous on the plane the following Tuesday that he could hardly sit still, prompting the woman seated next to him to ask if he had back trouble. He fumed at the woman behind the rental car desk when she took her own sweet time processing his paperwork. Once in the car, he drove like a maniac, breaking every speed limit on the way to Del Rosa and screeching into the driveway as if his sedate four-door sedan were a Ferrari.

Jill's jeep was gone, he realized with a crushing sense of disappointment. Parked in its place under the carport was a plain, late-model station wagon. Pauline must have a visitor, he decided. Rather than bothering his aunt while she entertained company, he skipped the formality of checking in with her first and headed straight for Jill's front door.

When no one answered his perfunctory knock, he boldly let himself in, intending to park himself on her sofa until she returned. The moment she walked through the door, he would sweep her into his arms and tell her all the things he'd stupidly held back, all the tender feelings he'd hidden, even from himself.

He'd taken maybe two steps into her living room when he skidded to a stop. Something was different. No, a *lot* of things were different, starting with the fact that the place was cleaned up. Her desk, now devoid of its decoration of pinned-up notes, boasted a brand-new personal computer. An instructional manual lay open next to the keyboard.

The scent of Jill's place was different, too. It wasn't nutmeg that greeted his nose on this visit, but the distinctive odor of...cinnamon? Or was that just his overactive imagination?

What was most different about Jill's apartment, however, was the lack of constant chirping. The finches were utterly quiet. One peek into the sun porch confirmed Stephen's suspicions—the little birds were gone. Not one single cage remained. Only the lovebirds were in evidence, occupying a place of honor on a stand by the sofa.

"What is going on?" he asked aloud.

The lovebirds shrieked at him, but he received no other answer.

Pauline would know. He cut through Jill's living room and dining room to the side door that led to the carport, and headed toward his aunt's kitchen. But just as his hand grasped the doorknob something in his peripheral vision caught his eye and drew him to a halt.

When he turned his head, the sight that greeted him drove the breath right from his body. Jill, wearing white gauzy slacks and a matching blouse, stood at the edge of the swimming pool, fishing out leaves with a long-handled net.

It *was* Jill, wasn't it? He had to blink his eyes several times to be sure. The long, racehorse legs were hers. The firm derriere, slender waist and softly rounded breasts were hers. But the hair! What had happened to her wild tangle of fiery cinnamon tresses? In its place was a neatly styled, chin-length bob.

Every romantic notion he'd had only moments before flew right out of his head as he strode toward her through the backyard.

"What the *hell* did you do to your hair?"

Chapter Ten

Jill dropped the pool skimmer from hands gone numb with astonishment. Surely this raving lunatic wasn't Stephen Whitfield. The cool, controlled, reserved Virgo man she knew would never bellow inane questions at her with such a lack of composure.

The clothes looked like Stephen. No one else could fill out a crisp pinstriped shirt and razor-creased trousers quite like he did. But one sleeve was uncharacteristically wrinkled, as if he'd slept on that arm during the flight to California, and his meticulously shined leather loafers bore faint spatters of mud. This impostor hadn't even stopped to have his shoes shined before leaving the airport.

"What do you think I did with my hair?" she finally replied, suppressing the silly grin that threatened to take hold of her face. He'd come back for her! She'd all but given up hope that he cared a whit about her, and she'd actually embarked on her own campaign to win him over. Now suddenly here he was! His unexpected presence was throwing her battle plan off schedule, but she was so elated to see him she didn't care.

Still, the beast was yelling at her and didn't appear at all pleased. He certainly didn't deserve any smiles from her, not yet.

"You cut it all off!" Stephen said, stating the obvious. "Why did you do that?"

"Why do you care?" she countered, suddenly defensive. "You never liked it, anyway. You said it looked like a mop."

"I said that?"

"Well, maybe you never said it in those words. But that's what you thought."

His chagrin was obvious as he averted his eyes. She imagined that only his well-practiced control prevented him from actually shuffling his feet. "Well I might have thought it was a little wild, but I never said I didn't *like* your hair. You must have cut six inches off."

"Eight, but who's counting?"

"And what happened to your finches? Your apartment sounds like a tomb without that constant undertone of chirping."

"I sold them all. They were taking up too much of my time, now that the spice business is off and running. I bought a computer, you know."

"Yes, I noticed."

"And I'm taking a class to learn how to use it. It's not as hard as I thought." And not as easy as Stephen would have had her believe, but she chose not to point that out.

"That's nice. Where's your jeep?" he asked sharply, seemingly unimpressed by her newfound business sense.

She shrugged. "The jeep wasn't very practical, especially since I was contemplating a cross-country road trip. I traded it in on a new—"

"You mean that sensible, sedate gray station wagon in the driveway is actually yours?"

She nodded, then wrinkled her nose. "But it's not gray. The color is called 'champagne.' It looks sort of pink when you see it in the sun. Don't you like it?" She felt the first stirrings of despair. Were all her hard-fought changes for nothing?

"The point is, do *you* like it? And what's this road trip you're talking about?"

"As long as I have to move, anyway, I decided to go back East and see my parents," she hedged, not quite ready to admit the whole truth, not yet. "I'll probably relocate permanently somewhere...a little closer to them. I didn't think I'd ever be saying this, but I actually miss them."

"Once you get out on your own, parents have a way of backing off and becoming almost human," Stephen agreed in a calmer tone of voice. But soon his frown returned abruptly, as if he'd just remembered something unpleasant. "You're digressing. Why all these sudden changes?"

"Because I felt like it!" she exploded, more and more uncomfortable with his scrutiny. Why had she jumped to the conclusion that he'd returned for her?

There could be a million reasons he was back in Del Rosa. "Stop giving me the third degree. Can't I make a few changes without upsetting everyone? And what are you doing here, anyway?"

"I, um, came to help Aunt Pauline prepare for her move." He sounded unsure of himself, and that was a first, as far as Jill could remember.

"I see," she responded, carefully mulling over her next gambit. They could stand out here all day, conversing but never saying anything. "I never had a chance to thank you for the lovebirds," she said, keeping her tone casual.

"Do you like them?" He sounded decidedly anxious. "I wasn't sure..."

"They're lovely, and very, um, talkative." *Noisy* described them more accurately. They fought more than they loved, reminding her of a certain other couple she knew. But she really didn't mind. Every time she heard them chortling, or even shrieking, she was reminded of the one romantic gesture Stephen had ever made toward her.

"Good, that's good." He stuffed his hands into his pockets. "Jill, I—"

"Stephen, I—"

They both started to talk at the same time, then halted self-consciously. He smiled and stared at the toes of his shoes, and she chuckled nervously.

"Go ahead," he said magnanimously.

Well, she'd been prepared to make the first move, anyway. Better here, on familiar home turf, than in Madison. "Stephen, surely you've figured it out by now. I made all the changes for you."

"Me?" He shook his head, as if he thought his hearing might be going bad.

"You like things to be orderly, logical and neat. So it was no wonder you had a hard time understanding and relating to me— I was disorganized, illogical and messy. I figured if there was to be any chance for me...for us...I would have to streamline myself and my life so I could fit into your life...somehow..."

Oh, Lord, she'd said too much. She'd sprung too much of a shock on him all at one time, judging from the look of extreme consternation on his face. Damn, she should have eased into the idea of a long-term relationship, not dumped it on him like a bucket of cold water.

But to her immense relief his gray eyes warmed, reminding her of gentle summer rain clouds, and he smiled like a little boy who'd been given a puppy for Christmas. He reached out and, with just one finger, barely touched her hair, where the ends stopped abruptly along her jawline. "You did this for me?"

She nodded uncertainly. "I was actually planning—well, thinking of moving to Madison once I got my life under control. I can run the spice business from any place, and even though California is great I really miss the fall leaves and the snow and the smell of a fire in the fireplace. Not that I wanted to move in with you or anything," she continued, because she was terrified of the silence that would follow her confession, "but I thought if I was just somewhere nearby where we could see each other and—"

"Why not move in with me?"

The question really threw her off. She opened her mouth to reply, but no words came out.

"I was just noticing, a few days ago, how big my house is and how empty it seems, and I was thinking, 'What this house needs is a bunch of noisy finches and the smell of nutmeg.' Boniface has been at loose ends since we went back, you know. He was so bored I considered importing a few mice, just to give him something to hunt."

"Oh, you considered no such thing. Stop teasing," she pleaded. "I was serious about moving to Madison, and you're making fun of me."

His tentative smile faded. "I'm sorry. I didn't intend to make light of you or your plans. I'm just a little overwhelmed, that's all, that you would go to such lengths to..." He touched her hair again, sending a shiver down her neck. "No pun intended."

"But you didn't even like me the way I was," she persisted.

He shook his head in denial. "I tried to convince myself I didn't. On the surface we do seem at odds with each other. But my heart didn't want to listen to logic. And well it shouldn't." He paused, taking a deep breath. "Jill, I didn't come back here just to help Aunt Pauline with her packing. I could have hired a moving company to do that. I came back because I love you."

"You do?" The whole backyard tipped crazily for a moment, and Jill actually wondered why all the water didn't slosh out of the pool.

"And I don't want you to try to change for me," he continued emphatically. "I love you exactly as you are—like a live wire, intense and unpredictable, and maybe just a wee bit disorganized. But you're also loving and generous and funny and... impulsive, dammit. I can't *believe* you cut your hair. Of all the crazy—you'd better grow it back out, and fast."

She opened her mouth to object, to tell him she'd shave her whole head if she wanted to and she didn't care *what* he thought. But of course she did care. He'd just told her he loved her, for heaven's sake, and there was nothing in the world she wanted more than to make him happy.

"Oh, Stephen!" That was all she could manage to say. She wanted to tell him that she loved him, too. He was the last person she would have expected to understand her, let alone accept her with all her myriad faults, and yet he did. He was the perfect foil for her innate craziness. He was her lighthouse in a storm, someone she could depend on always to keep her out of trouble and love her even when she made the most horrendous mistakes.

She wanted to tell him all of those things, but she couldn't quite form the words just now. So she kissed him instead, hoping he would understand even without the words. She put her hands on his wide shoulders and pulled him against her, raised her chin up and took what she wanted. He was going to have to get used to a bit of forwardness now and then, for when it came to loving, Jill was no shrinking violet who would wait for her man to come to her.

Judging from his enthusiastic reaction, he didn't mind. He laced his fingers through her hair—what was left of it—as his response turned to loving possession.

Never had a kiss felt so wonderful or said so much. It turned Jill inside out with longing, a longing made all the more sweet and poignant for knowing she would soon have what she craved.

"I must be crazy," he murmured against her ear, his warm breath sending shivers of delight shooting in every direction, "but I could swear you taste like cinnamon."

"You're not crazy. Cinnamon is December's spice of the month. I've got it all over me." She pulled away so she could look into his eyes, smiling as she took a step backward to balance herself. His answering smile again made her feel as if the ground beneath her feet had just dropped away with a dizzying abruptness, and she was falling...

But she really was falling—into the pool! She clutched at Stephen in a hopeless effort to catch herself, succeeding only in pulling him with her into the water. *This is it*, she thought during the brief seconds she was airborne. Those few moments of bliss were all she would get with Stephen. He might have forgiven her once for dunking him with his clothes on, but not twice.

They hit the surface of the pool with a loud *kersplatt*.

Hampered by the billowing gauze of her outfit, Jill clawed her way to the surface, sputtering and coughing when she finally reached life-giving air, though the prospect of drowning seemed only slightly less desirable than facing Stephen's certain wrath.

Strong arms slid around her middle, supporting her in the water. "Are you okay? Relax, I've got you. Here, you can stand up. It's not that deep."

"Omigosh I'm so sorry, Stephen," she said when she found her footing in the shoulder-deep water. "I can't believe how clumsy I am. Now I've ruined yet another set of your clothes." She tensed, waiting for the explosion.

"Don't worry, they're wash-and-wear," he said mildly, just before taking her in his arms and kissing her soundly again. He must have read her surprise in the feel of her kiss, because he pulled away, studying her thoughtfully—and for once, completely oblivious to his own disheveled state. Then the corner of his mouth turned up in amusement.

"You and Pauline are both Sagittarians," he said. "Are you going to be like her when you're her age?" he asked. The question seemed to come out of the blue.

"I certainly hope so," she answered sincerely. "I'd like to be as young at heart as she is when I'm seventy."

He nodded, seemingly satisfied. "And I'd like to stick around long enough to find out. Now, I know how you free-wheeling December women balk at the mere mention of permanent ties, but would you at least consider tying yourself down to an overorganized, controlling Virgo who loves you to distraction?"

"I—what did you say?"

"I'm asking you to marry me."

"Oh." Her heart started doing jumping jacks. "Ohhh. I'll certainly consider it," she quipped, trying to temper the rush of emotions that threatened to burst into the open. Permanent ties had never sounded better to *this* Sagittarian woman. Her next words were uttered with breathless certainty. "I'll consider it for about thirty seconds, and then I'll say yes."

It was a good thing his arms went around her then, because her shaky legs couldn't have held her up a moment longer, even in the water. He held her close, rocking gently back and forth. He didn't say anything, but he didn't have to.

"I should have known you'd want to do things up properly," she said when he released her some moments later, still struggling for breath and a little shaky as she tried to absorb the wonderful thing that had just happened. "It wouldn't do to have some crazy spice queen merely *living* with you. You have a formal church wedding in mind, no doubt?"

He frowned at that. "I had in mind an elopement. How does Tijuana sound?" At her gasp of surprise he added, "See, I can be impulsive, too. Besides, I could never wait all those months it would take to put a wedding together."

He was serious! She nodded happily, for once in perfect agreement with him. "We'll make the wedding toast with Margaritas," she murmured before he closed the space between them once again and kissed her to the depths of her soul.

In astrological terms their sun signs might add up to a challenging match. They would no doubt have their share of problems, starting with how to prevent Boniface from eating her lovebirds, once they all lived in the same house. But standing there in a swimming pool with Stephen, wrapped securely in his arms, Jill knew beyond a doubt they had all the love, passion, and patience they would need to sustain them through a lifetime of challenges.

* * * * *

LOVE AND THE VIRGO MAN

by Wendy Corsi Staub

The barefoot and fancy-free days of summer always make the superorganized Virgo man a little edgy. He breathes a huge sigh of relief when September rolls around, imposing schedules and structure once again. This hard-working fellow fills his daily appointment calendar from morning till night, which doesn't leave much room for mingling with the opposite sex. But September is "back to school" time, and a wife-hunting Virgo man might just decide to sign up for a continuing education course where he can learn something practical...and maybe meet the woman of his dreams!

In A CHANGED MAN, practical Virgo man Stephen Whitfield is bowled over when impulsive Sagittarius Jill Ballantine whirls into his life. Since she manages her own business, he'd probably find her in a night school course like Creative Bookkeeping for Entrepreneurs.

Which classes would the Virgo man take if he wanted to meet you?

The enterprising *Aries* woman is always looking for new ways to get tasks done quickly and efficiently, so she'll jump at the chance to take Computerize Your Home. By the time the semester is over, she'll be performing household duties with the push of a few buttons—leaving her more time to spend with her new Virgo beau!

The first name on the sign-up list for Baking With Chocolate is bound to be a *Taurus* woman; she adores sinfully rich treats! But cakes and cookies won't be her only temptation once she lays eyes on her handsome kitchen partner. From now on she'll be looking forward to what comes *after* dessert: sweet dreams about her irresistible Virgo man!

The intellectual *Gemini* woman wants to know *everything*, so Around the World in a Semester is the perfect course for her. Each night the class will focus on the culture, geography and history of a different country—and after class the attentive Virgo man will focus on *her!*

The *Cancer* woman appreciates artistic beauty, and she'll find out whether she has talent when she decides to take a Portrait Painting class. If she has a hard time capturing the handsome Virgo model on canvas, she's probably just distracted by the way he's looking at her. And when he suggests that they meet after class to "critique" her work, she won't hesitate to say yes!

The confident, flirtatious *Leo* woman is at the head of her Ballroom Dancing class, having mastered the old-fashioned steps with her spotlight-stealing style. When the debonair Virgo male cuts in, she'll melt in his arms, and her dance card will be off-limits to anyone else from that moment on!

The most likely place two *Virgos* would meet is at the Time Management seminar. They'll learn how to un-clutter their lives and will find themselves sharing organizational tips after class. Before long they'll realize that two can live as efficiently as one—and merge to form one happy, tidy household!

The *Libra* woman, with her inherent capability of seeing both sides of an issue, will be enthralled by a Famous American Trials class. When the students do a little role-playing to try a make-believe case, she'll be the most obvious choice to act as judge. She won't waste any time in ruling the Virgo man guilty—of first-degree flirtation!

The mystical *Scorpio* woman has always been fascinated by astrology, and she'll be on the edge of her seat in the Understanding Your Horoscope class. She'll discover that her sign is compatible with many others, but will decide it's fate that led her to sit beside a gorgeous Virgo...clearly *he* is her destiny!

LOVE AND THE VIRGO MAN

The levelheaded *Capricorn* woman might be all business when she signs up for Advanced Studies in Economics—but pleasure is waiting just around the corner. The pragmatic Virgo man is just as absorbed in the lectures as she is—but he'll have more than facts and figures on his mind when he asks her out for coffee afterward!

The environmentally conscious *Aquarius* woman is sure to be found not just enrolled in, but *leading* the Save the Earth discussion group. The nature-loving Virgo man will be her first volunteer when she organizes a neighborhood recycling plan—and love just might blossom as they sort paper and plastic side by side!

There's no doubt about it—the dramatic *Pisces* woman spends her evenings in the spotlight with the community theater group. The somewhat shy Virgo man might just overcome his stage fright to audition for a starring role in their latest production, just so he can romance his leading lady!

Silhouette
ROMANCE™

★ WRITTEN IN THE STARS ★

WHEN A LIBRA MAN MEETS A LIBRA WOMAN

Divorce attorney Jamison Marshall was willing to share everything with the lovely Blythe Reynolds—everything, that is, but his name. Now Blythe had to convince the stubborn, cynical—but lovable—man that even the best things in life are better when shared. ANYTHING BUT MARRIAGE by Tracy Sinclair is coming this October from Silhouette Romance. It's WRITTEN IN THE STARS!

Available in October at your favorite retail outlet, or order your copy now by sending your name, address, zip or postal code, along with a check or money order for $2.69 (please do not send cash), plus 75¢ postage and handling ($1.00 in Canada), payable to Silhouette Books to:

In the U.S.
3010 Walden Avenue
P.O. Box 1396
Buffalo, NY 14269-1396

In Canada
P.O. Box 609
Fort Erie, Ontario
L2A 5X3

Please specify book title with your order.
Canadian residents add applicable federal and provincial taxes.

SR1092

Take 4 bestselling love stories FREE

Plus get a FREE surprise gift!

Special Limited-time Offer

Mail to Silhouette Reader Service™

In the U.S.	In Canada
3010 Walden Avenue	P.O. Box 609
P.O. Box 1867	Fort Erie, Ontario
Buffalo, N.Y. 14269-1867	L2A 5X3

YES! Please send me 4 free Silhouette Romance™ novels and my free surprise gift. Then send me 6 brand-new novels every month, which I will receive months before they appear in bookstores. Bill me at the low price of $2.25* each—a savings of 44¢ apiece off the cover prices. There are no shipping, handling or other hidden costs. I understand that accepting the books and gift places me under no obligation ever to buy any books. I can always return a shipment and cancel at any time. Even if I never buy another book from Silhouette, the 4 free books and the surprise gift are mine to keep forever.

*Offer slightly different in Canada—$2.25 per book plus 69¢ per shipment for delivery. Canadian residents add applicable federal and provincial sales tax. Sales tax applicable in N.Y.

215 BPA ADL9　　　　　　　　　　　　　　　　　　　　　　　　　　　　315 BPA ADMN

Name _____ (PLEASE PRINT)

Address _____ Apt. No. _____

City _____ State/Prov. _____ Zip/Postal Code _____

This offer is limited to one order per household and not valid to present Silhouette Romance™ subscribers. Terms and prices are subject to change.

SROM-92　　　　　　　　　　　　　　　　　　　© 1990 Harlequin Enterprises Limited

HE'S MORE THAN A MAN, HE'S ONE OF OUR

Dear Christina,

Stationed here in the Gulf, as part of the peacekeeping effort, I've learned that family and children are the most important things about life. I need a woman who wants a family as much as I do....

Love, Joe

Dear Joe,

How can I tell you this...?

Love, Christina

Dear Reader,

Read between the lines as Toni Collins's FABULOUS FATHER, Joe Parish, and Christina Holland fall in love through the mail in LETTERS FROM HOME. Coming this October from

Silhouette
R O M A N C E™

FFATHER2